All
The
Women
She
Knows

About Tutku Barbaros

Tutku is a writer – across forms – of Turkish Cypriot heritage from south-east London. She is an alumna of the Royal Court Writers' Programme as well as Sphinx Theatre's year-long writer's development programme, Sphinx 30. Her play *Layla and Youssef* was longlisted for the Bruntwood Prize and the Paines Plough Women's Prize For Playwriting. Tutku also leads creative writing workshops.

All the Women She Knows is her debut collection of short stories.

About Dear Damsels

Dear Damsels is a community and platform supporting women writers through free and inclusive opportunities to write together. Since 2016, DD has published five empowering collections of fiction, non-fiction and poetry and shared the words of hundreds of women.

www.deardamsels.com

Tutku Barbaros

All
The
Women
She
Knows

First published in Great Britain in 2024 by Dear Damsels

2

ISBN 978-1-8381-6613-7

Printed and bound in Great Britain by Clays Ltd, Elcograf S.p.A.

Dear Damsels
www.deardamsels.com

Dear Damsels gratefully acknowledges that our work is supported using
public funding by Arts Council England.

Supported using public funding by
**ARTS COUNCIL
ENGLAND**

Contents

Notes on Content

Rey Was Taught
Death, anxiety

Clea and the Playsuit
Body image, diet culture, eating disorders

Rey Walks into a Hair Salon
Death

Magenta Moves In
Domestic abuse

Dia is a Leader
Body image, diet culture, sexual assault, miscarriage

Rey Goes on a Journey
Death

A Wedding in Full Swing
Death

Rey Was Taught

that complex times call for simple pleasures. These are the words
Rey's mother had said.

So today, to calm her restless hands and ease her shaky breath,
She says to herself again and again,
'Look, here's a thing to be grateful for and another, and another.'
Referring to overnight oats she made last night, in the knowledge
she would feel like this today.
Referring, also, to opening a fresh tub of moisturiser and being
greeted with a cocoa-butter peak so fluffy it reminded her of count-
less whippy ice creams enjoyed as a child.
Rey's was always hundreds and thousands and a drizzle of blue
bubblegum sauce.
Her mum's was lemon sorbet with a drizzle of strawberry, maybe
a flake.

Enjoyed on the doorstep of their house, as they watched the ice cream truck chug away, wishing the ice cream man a good day.

Rey is also grateful, this morning, that her favourite, usually elusive, not too loose but not too tight scrunchie is in the place she left it (and not moved around by the mystic forces that enjoy relocating her diary and phone charger).

Rey pulls her curls off her face,
gathers them high above her head,
and allows herself to walk a few inches taller.

Maybe, just maybe, she tells herself, today will be okay.

She repeats the words out loud, until she finds a rhythm, until they're something she can sing. Her voice comes together like brownies in a pan, initially disparate and grainy before turning into something irresistible, something glossy, something that fills a void, creates comfort.

> 'Maybe, just maybeee
> Today will be okaaay
> Maybe, just maybeee
> Todaaay will be okaaay.'

She does this often. She also sings songs about the dinner while she's cooking it. Making up lyrics about the papayas and the aubergines.

> 'Floating about in a tomato seaaaaa
> Oh what a life the garlic leads!'

Tapping rhythms onto the surfaces of the kitchen with ladles, nudging cupboards shut with a bump of her hips. Rey believes she is in a world of her own but Sal, the landlady, the type of woman who owns a lot of silk robes and wears a lot of beads, lives in the flat below and often leaves her window open, listening out for signs of Rey. For Sal, it's like living in a constant musical. She listens because she cares but also because she's a bit nosey.

Sal's ears await today's opening number as she prunes the herbs in the box on her balcony. Rey sings:

'We're gonna seeeee Mel

I hope it goes well
    I've packed up his things
        like saying goodbye twice.
We're gonna see Mel,
    Better make sure we look nice.'

Sal nods and sets about pre-emptively plucking mint leaves for a brew to soothe Rey when she returns from meeting up with her ex.

Upstairs Rey packs a canvas bag.
A bag formerly known as 'The Clubbing Bag', because in the early days when there was always a pizza in the oven and sambuca in the shot glasses, Rey and Mel would go out out. They and their mates would face the Brighton winds and queue for clubs that line the beach. Once inside they'd strip off their coats, stuff them in their bag and pay a pound to have it stowed away so they could dance. And dance Rey did.

She would throw her entire body into the music and she'd throw it incredibly well.

Throwing herself hard enough to the beat that for a minute or two she might forget her grief.

And sometimes she had tears in her eyes.

And most times no one saw.

Now, sat cross-legged on the floor (she's been working on her posture) Rey goes through the beer-stained, frayed bag one last time. It sags with the weight of their relationship inventory. Mostly books. Thin ones only of course, because they both agree a book shouldn't be too big or too heavy.

Mel is one of those people who really lives with his books, shoving them into rucksacks and back pockets.

Whereas as Rey requires a reading nook, a special place she and her book can go to, with soft blankets, chocolate and a glass of red wine she chooses solely because of the description on the bottle: 'sweet and smooth', 'bouncy and floral'.

Because of their differing reading habits, it's easy to tell which book belongs to who. Rey recoils at this particular one, which has evidently been dropped, at least twice, in the bath. Poor thing truly looks like it's been through it, she thinks. She flicks to the back page because Mel likes to write a note about if the ending works or not. However, in this book, under the last sentence, is a question.

I'm not sure. . . Rey, what do you think???

She hasn't got round to reading it, and now it's too late.

Rey eats peanut butter directly from the jar as she contemplates the magnets on the fridge door.

She takes down the ones they picked up on the pier: photos of them hurtling down a log flume.

Mel is grinning and his arms are flailing but there's nothing behind Rey's eyes.

She remembers those days being among her numbest.

Six months into the relationship when Mel's efforts to cheer her up had become too elaborate.

Rey recalls existential dread at the group mini-golf trip and feeling suffocated at the pub quiz.

It wasn't long before she started sneaking off without saying good-bye. Sending a text from the bus.

She takes the t-shirts of his she's washed and dried, places the magnets in the middle of them and folds them up so nothing more can break.

She holds it all in her hands, a parcel and a time capsule.

Hanging by the door is the ochre scarf she started knitting for him in an attempt to placate his incessant complaining about the cold flat. The argument that meant she put the project down still rings in her ears. Mel demanding:

'You're such a people pleaser – you won't even complain to your landlady about how fucking cold your flat is, Rey. What else will you suffer?'

She squeezed the ball of wool tightly in her hands and hoped Sal hadn't heard. It was in those moments Rey regretted asking Mel to move in at all. She'd only suggested it so she'd have someone to be with at 3 a.m. I moved him into my space far too fast, she says to herself now as she applies lip balm and pulls on jeans.

In the mirror by the door, she sees her khaki shirt is inside out. She hears her nan's voice in her head (her warning it's bad luck to correct clothes unless you spin three times first).

The title of an essay she wrote pops into her head ('To Wish the Magpie Good Morning: On the Language of Superstition') then pops out. She locks the door, double checks she's locked the door, and steps out with all her seams on display.

Every time Rey walks down her street with its tall pastel pink-and-buttercream-yellow buildings trailing behind her like angel cakes, she's reminded why she left London to be here:

the sea, the sea, the sea.

The way the salt air sweeps into her lungs. The foamy tide that fills her ears. Matte-grey, shiny-black and denim-blue pebbles rolling beneath her sturdy lace-up boots.

When she gets to the cafe, she's unsettled to see a usually late Mel is already there. Typical. Now he can be on time, she chides to herself, at the memory of missing the opening scene of many plays. He's sat on the terrace, head down, deep in a book, butterscotch hair tied loosely at the nape of his neck. She does still like that about him: the way he looks like a surfer while being practical like a fisherman.

She sits down strategically so there's no opportunity for a hug. It's been so long since she's allowed anyone to hold her, she feels genuinely unsure as to how she might react. A part of her worries she might forget, feel too comfortable and rest her head against Mel's chest. She imagines Mel appalled and shaking her off.

An image he immediately betrays with the smile he now offers her:

'Hello you,' he says.

'Hey hey,' she says.

By the time she's exhaled in unbridled relief at managing to sound normal, the waiter is asking her order. Such haste would usually irritate Rey but today it helps.

She orders an oat-milk latte.

Mel, an expensive lemonade.

Lemonade is a terrible choice, thinks Rey. How can you have a conversation over lemonade?

She imagines it arriving with a tag that says 'drink me'.

She imagines Mel growing one million, two million times his size. Perhaps if he does that, she thinks, he can go to the house, and hug it until his body heat warms it up, and maybe then he'll be happy.

When the drink arrives Mel greets it with an 'oh for fuck's sake'.

'What?' asks Rey. 'It's what you ordered?'

He picks up the straw and waves it in a fury. 'Paper straw. Paper dickhead straw.'

Rey shrugs and says, 'They're better for the environment!' but Mel refuses to let this go. 'Yeah but they always fall apart after about one sip. They're literally not designed to get wet'. He resigns himself to puckering his lips around the straw in a bid to keep it dry.

Mel looks so bizarre that Rey does something she didn't expect to do today: she laughs.

Rey had always revelled in the injustices Mel felt in relation to menial things.

Sometimes it made her wish she was him.

Or at least that those things were the biggest of her worries too.

'Maybe you should get one of those stainless steel ones?' Rey suggests.
'I have thought about that y'know, but where do you keep 'em?'
'In your pencil case?'
'I haven't used a pencil case in ten years and even so I don't think that's massively hygienic.'
'Hmm, ok. . . err. . .'
'It's okay, you don't have to solve it, babe.'

The part of Rey that lights up when Mel calls her babe battles for attention with the part of Rey that has to solve this straw problem.

'Toothbrush guard?'
'That's not a bad idea.'

Rey can't tell if Mel is just humouring her. Before she has a chance to push the topic further, he asks carefully:

'So. You doing much writing?'
'Truthfully, work is mad busy so my focus is there. It's nice though; working from home.'
'God! That's going to be freezing once winter hits.'

Mel is clearly still furious at her for swapping the fantasy of lounging on the sofa bathed in British seaside light for the reality of bundling up in two duvets day and night, but she doesn't know what to say to him. She also doesn't want to disappoint him, so she claims she's been trying to write when she hasn't.

It's funny though, thinks Rey, her mum had always remarked what a terrible liar Rey is and yet Mel doesn't seem suspicious at all. Instead, he notices a ring he's not seen before:

'That one's new.'

He gestures to the filigree gold on her index finger. Wedged among the rings on every other finger.

'I got it after you. . . after we. . . err. . . I don't wanna say "dumped me". That sounds so cruel. But. . . yeah. . .'

'Don't say that. Not dumped. Not that word. . . let's say. . . after I ended the relationship. . . as we know it. . . like romantically.'

Rey rolls her eyes: he still thinks they can be friends.

At that, the couple on the neighbouring table, tilt their heads closer so as to listen in. Rey knows why. She can practically feel their 'ohhhh woooow gosh they're exes? Didn't see that coming, they do not look like lovers.' And the truth is, they don't and never did.

As he waves the waiter back over, she notices the series of festival wristbands on Mel's arm and accidentally says out loud,

'Well, someone had a good summer?'
'Yeah, well. . .' He says guiltily at first, but then, she watches in real time as his guilt turns to a defiant look of '*why should I feel bad about this?*' before fading into a need to appear casual.
He asks 'What about you, been away this summer?'

And Rey replies 'Nah, just simple pleasures'.
And he sighs. That 'simple pleasures' thing again.

If she said it to rile him (and maybe she did – frankly, she's not sure anymore) it hasn't worked, because to her surprise the waiter arrives and, instead of the bill, Mel orders a pot of ginger tea. He asks her if she wants some too and she says yes even though she despises the idea of going from one drink to another.

When the waiter's gone Rey asks:

>   'What's the story with the tea? You used to have a coffee a minute.'

>   'Oh, it's just decaf life innit. . . helps with the anxiety.'

'The anxiety'. He always said it like that, the way others talked about their partners with a wink and an air of 'oh to be young, free and single'. The way someone might say they'd better leave the pub because 'the old ball and chain' is at home, waiting. And actually that is accurate, because anxiety is, in so many ways, the other half of him. He never, ever misses a therapy session.

>   'That's interesting,' says Rey.
>   'Yeah. I couldn't stay on eight cups a day. I was getting palpitations. It was doing me in.'
>   'Was it?'
>   'Yeah. I told you, Rey. . .'
>   'Did you?'
>   'I mean come on, you were there. It was exacerbating

everything. I was wired, not sleeping, shaking constantly. . . I told you all this. . . I told you that day. . .'

Rey wants to say, 'I wasn't listening Mel. . . I was watching the kettle steam roll up the walls. . . and preparing myself to be alone' but instead she escapes to the bathroom, runs the water until it's icy and places her wrists under the tap until the flurry in her calms.

Waiting for her at the table is the ginger tea in a glass pot. It's resplendent, bigger than she expected – essentially a fishbowl. Slivers of ginger lay like languid ribbons beneath shimmering columns of lemongrass. Fine slices of orange float on the surface. Each citrus segment splits the light like a golden kaleidoscope. It looks like treasure to Rey. It reminds her of the fruit salads at the buffet birthdays of her favourite auntie, the one who always encouraged her to write stories.

'I knew that would make you smile! It's nice, innit?'
'It is – it's gorgeous.'

Rey thinks that this would probably be a good moment to touch his hand but then he says,

'All your favourite colours!'

And something in Rey jolts. Because the thing is. It's not. It's beautiful. Without a doubt it's beautiful. Rey knows that. But it's not her favourite colours at all. She feels a flood of disbelief that he doesn't know this. Okay, they were only together for year and a bit, but. . . she wants to play a belated game of Mr and Mrs because she's aching to know who exactly he thinks she is.

She's angry at him for not knowing the simplest of things.

But then that anger breaks like a wave inside her because she knows it's not fair.

Because she knows it's not his fault.

Because when she met him, she wasn't herself. It was only months after her mum had died. He has no idea who she was before that seismic grief. And neither of them has any idea who she is now.

Mel knows, from the way her brown eyes glow as she undoes her hair, crunches her curls in her hands and then re-ties her hair, that he's got something wrong. He knows she's plummeting inside herself, the way she did most days before. Where another person might get up and go, tired of never knowing what to say or do with someone who retreats like this, Mel is the kind of man who can be patient.

They watch the tea as it cools enough that they might drink it. Eventually Mel pours.

'Holiday mugs,' says Rey wistfully.

'Huh?' responds Mel.

'They. . . these glasses. . . remind me of holidays. What you'd get in a villa, not that I've stayed in many villas but yeah. . . or. . . well, actually, they remind me of. . . my nan's place in Cyprus, she had loads like this. And them traditional ones that are shaped like tear drops.'

Rey has mentioned her family to Mel perhaps three times. He holds both hands around the glass and hopes for just a little more.

'Your mum's mum?'

'Yeah, my mum's mum.'

But Rey can't say more. In her mind she sees herself opening the kitchen cupboard of her London house and seeing the cups there too. After a while Mel suggests 'Shall we pretend we're on holiday?' Rey lets out a troubled laugh and says: 'I think I've done enough running from the truth already Mel.'

In the silence a seagull soars past and beaks a tuna melt from the plate of a child who shrieks so loudly several passers-by stop in their tracks. Rey and Mel both do a startled laugh, and both feel instantly guilty about it (the child is very upset). The fact they then try to resume seriousness actually makes them laugh genuinely, gently. Rey allows Mel to rest his eyes on hers and says:

'I'm sorry I never showed you the real me, Mel.'

And without a pause, he says:

'Well as long as you know who the real Rey is that's all that matters.'

They both go to start new sentences, or maybe old sentences, and stop. Neither of them knows exactly what to say and it's hard to know exactly how much time is passing between them but it feels right to honour the silence just a little longer. To let it sit. To stop forcing themselves to fill it the way they did before. When Rey's phone bleeps to say it's running out of battery. Mel still automatically reaches into his bag and connects it to his charger. As he does so he says, 'This is solar powered by the way' and Rey cuts him off, jokingly. 'So you do care about the environment after all?!' He takes the bait. 'Of course, I care about the environment, how could you say that? What I'm getting at is it's slow as fuck. . . so like. . . do you fancy something to eat? Dunno about you, but I could smash a veggie breakfast. . . ?'

A part of Rey wishes their life was an open document on the screen. She imagines scrolling across the last eighteen months, highlighting, selecting all and then deleting everything just after their first sentence. When Rey met Mel at a friend's BBQ on Brighton beach. When he couldn't find a bottle opener she opened his beer with her teeth. And he said, 'That was presumptuous, now your spit's all on my bottle,' and she replied with a kiss.
Which was incredibly out of character.
A first impression she regrets making.
Because really all she wanted was to be held.
All she needed, really needed, was a friend.
She imagines how things might have been different if she'd gone back to London and spent time with the people that had known her for her whole life instead of pretending to be someone who was completely fine. She also hears Sal's frequent warnings, that she can't go back in time, that life is too short for regrets and that she has to learn and move on instead.

Rey draws the conversation to end. She says she has somewhere she needs to be and in a way that's true but she's not sure where.

Mel picks up The Clubbing Bag and has a brief look through its contents. He fishes out the battered paperback with the undecided footnote at the end and says:

'No, no – I left that on purpose, I still really need to know what you thought about it.'

Rey takes the book and says she'll read it as soon as she gets a chance. Mel wisely opts not to force a hug and instead places a friendly grip on Rey's shoulders as he says, 'Good! And in the meantime, don't be a stranger.' Rey wants to say 'bit late for that,' but smiles instead and watches as he walks away.

*

On her way home Rey stops to watch the sky.
Clouds rushing past as though they have somewhere to be,
She longs to know where they're off to, and why they have to leave.
The sun sets orange as the ginger tea and the world, for a minute, feels like infinite colours.
She wishes she didn't feel so lost: the stones, the sea, the light, she keeps telling herself she still adores it. But increasingly she feels nothing. She knows something is missing.

When she gets home she picks up a pen and continues to write her gratitude list. Just as she settles into this Sal calls up to her:

'Rey, love, are you in there? This came to me, but it's addressed to you! Look's fancy!'

The envelope does look fancy. Glossy rather than matte. Rey's name written in bronze letters. When she opens it, she sees it's an invitation to a wedding. One of the girls from school.

'Oh wow, that looks like it'll be fun! Oh and you'll get to dress up and maybe there'll be men there? Oh, I love a wedding.'
'Yeah. Can't imagine I'll go.'

This exasperates Sal.

'Why's that?'
'It will mean going to London and I don't really want to do that,' replies Rey flatly.

Rey sees Sal's annoyance and knows it's informed by the life Sal has lived. A juicy life. Sal doesn't have regrets, but she certainly has stories. Stories she's told Rey. Adventurous ones. Sexy ones. The kind of stories that drip from your tongue. She goes away frequently, deciding on Monday she'd like to be somewhere else entirely by Wednesday. Sal always returns having acquired more and more friends from more and more places. She hosts guests frequently. Drags Rey downstairs to meet them over drinks and snacks. Rey knows she's always trying to make a match. Rey is certain that were she to move out, the house would become a bustling party-throwing hotel.

But, her usual frivolity aside, Sal says, seriously now,

'Don't you think you deserve a good time, Rey?'
'I'm cool just sticking with life's smaller treats. I don't need to go to a big fancy wedding.'

'Ah yes "Complex times call for simple pleasures."'

Rey bristles – she doesn't like hearing her mum quoted back at her like this.

Sal takes a breath before saying something she's wanted to say for a while.

'Rey, sweetheart. Excuse me for being blunt. . . but. . . Lord knows that floppy-haired Mel isn't going to spit it out. Your mum only said that to you because at that time she was unwell, she was making the most of a horrid situation and helping you do the same. But now… you should be doing more than muddling along, sweetheart. I'm sure this isn't what your mum would have wan–'

Before Sal can get the word 'wanted' out, Rey interrupts her.

'Alright,' says Rey. 'It's been a long enough day already. . .'

Rey motions to the door and Sal takes her cue to go.

Rey picks up the invitation. Runs her hands over each familiar word. The RSVP will go to the road she grew up on. Will fall through the letterbox of the house with all the lavender in the garden. She remembers hours and hours sat in that living room. She remembers her own living room too. She can't see all those people she hasn't seen since the funeral. She goes to write she won't be attending because she can't, just can't, go home. But her hand stops.

That night Rey, Mel and Sal don't sleep.

In the morning Sal is banging on the door again.

'Wake up! I've got something fun for us!'

Rey is tentative – 'something fun' could mean literally anything from Sal. She half expects to see penguins liberated from a zoo or an invitation to an orgy. Rey beams when Sal presents a Turkish coffee set gifted to her by a friend just back from their holidays.

Sal throws herself on the sofa and watches as Rey prepares the coffee. Rey can't remember the last time she did this but the memory of how to, lives deep in her muscles. Don't let it boil over. Something in Rey starts to wake up.

When they've finished drinking, Rey turns her cup upside down into the saucer and motions to Sal to do the same before explaining, 'let's give it a bit of time to settle and then I'll tell you all your fortunes. . . okay? I know you absolutely live for this stuff.' Rey enjoys indulging Sal. Perhaps it will make up for being rude last night she thinks, before apologising. 'I'm so sorry I snapped at you yesterday, Sal.' Sal fondly chuckles. 'Oh, Rey. Snap? You call that a snap? Honestly, I WISH you'd snap once in a while!'

After Rey has narrated the birds, journeys, and messages in Sal's cup (to Sal's unending delight), Sal deems herself to be understanding the symbols too, so reaches for Rey's cup.
But in Rey's cup the coffee has barely budged, it's remained solid at the base.
Rey knows this represents her past. Her family. Her sadness.

Rey knows if she was sitting here with an aunty, they'd be lamenting how much stress Rey is holding, how stuck she is. She can hear the specific Turkish word they'd be using.

Sıkıntı.

No dots above the I, thinks Rey.

Later on, when Sal has gone and Rey clears the cups away, she sees the coffee sediment has remained stubborn. Obstinate. She mutters to it in Turkish. It mutters something back, and deep in her heart she knows that the coffee is right, she needs to stop trying to read her future. She needs to start writing it.

She looks around the flat, hears the sea in the distance and wishes she could hear traffic. She thinks about the person she's been in these walls and the person she hasn't been, too. She thinks about London. About her mum's house. About how a home can be so empty but so full at the same time. Like her.

She thinks about this wedding. It's a long way off, the date on the card feels a million years away but a sense starts to rattle through her.

Maybe she could go?

A knowing blows her open.

Maybe she could ease herself back into London?

She sees their street in her mind.

It's agonising and it's brilliant.

It confronts her and it demands that she confront it in return.

She doesn't want to be stranded at the bottom of the cup forever.

She doesn't want to be lost to grief's inertia.

She imagines herself getting ready for the wedding, knowing people there will remember the person she used to be.

And maybe it's good that people there will have known her mum. Maybe that's what she needs.

She picks up the invitation, and admits to herself her mum would have really wanted to go.

So she has to.

She's heard other people talk like this, about those moments in life that feel right, like the time is definitely now. And without a second thought she follows that feeling.

She starts to pack her things. Pulling her clothes off the rail and into her suitcase. She's half tempted to leave it all there and just go right then and there.

She looks around and says 'I want more than this. So much more than this.'

She hums the words quietly to herself.

> 'It's time to go home.
>> It's time to go home.
>>> Rey, it's time to go home.'

She swears the wind is singing along: not begging her to stay but sending her on her way. She can't imagine a single thing harder than going home. But she can't imagine going on longer like this either. She can't keep living on her knees while thanking the ground for holding her up.

The next day she gives her notice to Sal, who says 'thank fuck' as she wipes a tear from her eye and wishes Rey the absolute greatest of luck.

Taffy and the Joint

Taffy has done her knee in. She's not sure exactly how, possible bad luck, perks of her waitressing job. But then there's also the years of kicking about, skipping beats, running late. Her GP, a caring woman, Doctor Kind Eyes let's call her, on account of the caring way she looks at her, detailed the way Taffy's connective tissue is out of whack – well, not in so many words – but something like that.

She booked Taffy an MRI. Taffy has always had this thing about them. This concern that the machine will swallow her whole. Obviously, instead of just expressing that, Taffy makes jokes about how she thinks having an MRI must be like being a butt plug shoved up a giant robot arse. Doctor Kind Eyes just looks at her, unsure whether or not to laugh.
She does laugh eventually, in the end, because she's polite, trained, empathetic: is aware that fear can often wear a jokey guise.

She comforts her, agreeing that yes, come to think of it, it does sound like a pneumatic drill clashing into all the metal of the world, but it's done now and Taffy should be proud of herself because Taffy did it even though Taffy was scared.

Taffy bats off the praise. But remembers distinctly saying the same thing to herself in the hospital as she rid herself of the blue gown, and returned her piercings to their rightful places. At least it's done now. At least that bit is done now.

With one hand on the keyboard and the other on a pen, Doctor Kind Eyes asks Taffy if she's sleeping, how's her eating, if she's stressed. She's asking her *again*.

Taffy shares a lukewarm sentence or two, saying that she's fine. But it doesn't take a medical degree to know that that's a burning lie. Trying a different angle, Doctor Kind Eyes pulls up Taffy's notes again, asks 'are you still in a band?'

'I am' says Taffy.
'That must be intense.
Is it ever over stimulating would you say?
Do you get stage fright?
Post-show blues?
Do you ever feel overwhelmed by financial uncertainty?
Have you had any more panic attacks since the last one?
Are you still taking those supplements, the iron?'

Taffy offers shallow answers to important questions and the doctor sighs, stresses again, that physio will help, but maybe not just physio alone? 'Would you like to talk about anything?'

Taffy shuts the question down. 'It's fine, no thank you, no.'

And with that, Taffy's tab on the computer is closed.

Taffy finds herself begrudgingly pushed through the capillaries of the system.

Because the thing is, she can't keep shoving this under the carpet: sometimes bits of her cartilage chip off and sometimes those little bits of cartilage wedge themselves between the joints of her knee and they leave her stuck. This time, sofa-bound. Sometimes, for up to a week.

She can't ignore this anymore.

She's got shit to do.

She buys a blow-up parrot from the pound shop and posts about it. 'Peg Leg of Peckham', she calls herself. With a witticism about why would birds be comfortable going, with pirates, to sea? That afternoon she receives a letter with her first appointment date.

She's nervous about it. Like, really nervous. Not so nervous that she doesn't note the irony of there being no lift to a physio department on the third floor. But nervous enough.

The cartilage is fine at the minute. She's going to have to explain that, and she will probably feel like an idiot

and and and

maybe this is actually all just a big faff?!

(She always feels like she's taking up someone else's precious time. She feels guilty all the time.)

Then, along the corridor, there's a painting of sunflowers on the door.

And that makes her feel calmer more capable as she takes her seat.

A stacked man enters the waiting room, and she snorts because obviously he has a reason to be there – he clearly does sports so that makes sense – that is how one achieves a sports injury. It really is a case of damned if you do lots of exercise, damned if you don't do any exercise at all.

She's filling in the form she's been handed with intense focus when an Irish accent calls her name,
startled, she drops her water bottle.
Watching in disgust, as it rolls across the floor
she wants to leave it there
because the thought of all the germs it's picked up turns her stomach
but that would look weird, so she chases and then grabs it
(which also looks weird)
From a crouched position on the floor, she sees the body attached to the accent.
His eyebrows raised jovially, he asks, 'Hand-eye coordination a problem, then?'
She responds saying hand-eye coordination is fine.
As is he, she notes silently.
Fine, with several 'I's
Fiiiii-iiiiiii-iiiiiiiine.

As usual the bed is just that little bit too high so she begins weighing up the best strategy to mount it.
His eyes search her face.

'Sorry! I was thinking about how to mount the thing, sorry.'
'Mount the what, sorry?'
'The. . .uhm. . .' She slaps the bed.
'Oh right, the bed! Sorry!'

She says something about how she wouldn't really classify that as
a bed, and he agrees. They settle on it being a bit more of a table
as he lowers it for her. It being adjustable is something she's never
considered. Intrusive memories of her naked fanny clambering onto
the 'bed' while a beautician pretends to get the wax pot ready rush
to her mind before suddenly, she feels him observing her again.
She has a sip of water.
As she swallows she remembers the pilgrimage of lurgy her bottle
recently embarked on.
The physio grimaces with her, which is not reassuring at all.

He cracks up laughing.
She joins him there.

She's on her back now as he assesses the range of her knee
gently pushing it closer and closer towards her torso,
continually asking if it hurts, which it doesn't.
Eventually the knee is pressed up against her chest. Well, not her
chest: her tits.
She makes a joke about that.
About how when she looks at other women doing yoga their bodies
form straight lines, they look like a zig zag, like a very neat isosceles
triangle.
She's all boobs and bum, she says.

She always feels out of kilter, feels scalene almost all the time she says.

He laughs, 'Scalene is absolutely fine' he says,

adding 'does yoga' to his notes.

Tells her that it's working: she's very flexible.

'I know' she says.

The thin blue paper sticks to the sweat in the small of her back, she jokes that when she gets up it will form a kind of cape.

'I reckon you could pull that off,' he says.

The grunting of a 75-year-old trying to touch his toes on the other side of the curtain interrupts their brief silence.

They laugh again.

Returning to his list, he goes over the notes about her weight and height.

For both of which Taffy attempts to apologise.

They talk about a lot
    while he's shoving her legs around, working out what's
improving, what isn't.
    Flitting between necessary questions, a kind of curi-
osity and increasingly familiar instructions.
Because it's necessary for the healing
over the weeks she has to reveal a lot to him.

Her band, carrying amps, no time to rest, jumping on and off stage, gig, gig, gig, no boyfriend, no girlfriend either, the part-time jobs, she's good at waiting tables, crap at making coffee. He says it could be exacerbated by stress, gently asks what profits she makes, and she says 'profits' are a stretch.

And they talk about that.

He asks her to place her heel on his hand and push him away as hard as she can.
He mentions he loves festivals. Names some he's been to. They've been in a lot of the same places.
She lets out heavy sigh.

    'Did that hurt, where? Here? Why?'
    'No,' she says.
    'Yes,' she thinks, 'I wish I'd met you anywhere but here.'

She'd love to say it but knows she can't.
Instead, she just keeps pushing her heel hard into the base of his palm.

The next week he announces they're doing something different. She hopes it's a pint at the pub. He leads her out to the bigger sports room. Blindfolds her. Guides her onto a wobbly thing and throws beanbags at her. To improve her coordination apparently.
They fill the space with laughter,
laughter that bounces off the apparatus and echoes through them both, bouncing freely in the space between them.
Off balance she stumbles, let's out an almighty 'FUCKKK' – terrified she'll crack her head open.
He catches her (obviously),
    turns out he's standing really really close (obviously)

'I've got you,' he says.

I wish, she thinks.

She's about to go on tour and she's nervous. He talks her through it, and when she struggles to comprehend, he demonstrates instead. You need to bend your knee like this, gently rotate your leg like that and elevate it if it gets painful. Ice is always good. She watches his body. Tries to stay with his words. With authority, he promises,

'It shouldn't lock up anyway, I think you should be okay.'

As we know though, shouldn't isn't the same as won't. She should not give him a flyer for her show, but that doesn't mean she will not. He takes it, flattered, pretends this isn't wholly inappropriate, folds it up and pops it in his pocket, presumably so no other practitioners clock it.

While away on tour, she accidentally misses her last appointment.
Gets taken off the patient list.
And that is it.
    She wonders if he's offended. If he feels stood up.
    Reminds herself he could have turned up.
She presumes they live in the same borough,
            maybe they'll run into each other?
She has to do the exercises every day.
So, of course, she thinks about him every time.

Months later, she's back with Doctor Kind Eyes, assessing the knee situation.

Taffy's thinking about all the cheeky winks, all the fascination. With one hand on the keyboard and the other on a pen, Doctor Kind Eyes asks her if she's sleeping, how's her eating, if she's stressed?

Taffy remembers the heel of her foot pushing into the palm of his hand.

Taffy remembers trusting someone new.

Doctor Kind Eyes repeats,

'Are you sleeping? How's your eating? Would you say you're stressed?'

Taffy rests a hand on her healing knee, a part of herself she's learning to understand.

Doctor Kind Eyes begins to wrap things up, but Taffy isn't getting up to go.

That palm on her heel was like setting off a line of dominoes.

His touch set her on a new path.

She answers,

'No, I'm not sleeping, and it's making everything really, really, hard. Sometimes I'm so exhausted I cry. And also, I lied, sorry. I said I hadn't had any more panic attacks, but I have. So yes, I am stressed. And also, in the interest of transparency, I never even finished the course of physio. I don't even know why. I just dropped the ball, beanbag, I guess. But I am eating! I never have a problem with eating, as you can see!'

Doctor Kind Eyes' hands leave the keyboard and the pen, meet in the middle, clasping, joined.

She's relieved.

'Okay. Let's talk about the sleeping first. Do you feel ready to be connected to someone who can help?'

'Yes, I'm ready,' Taffy says with terror in her eyes, 'yes' she says again. 'I think it's time.'

Clea and the Playsuit

A red playsuit on a rack,
Will safely hold a body.
A heart
Let you run for the bus
Dance all night,
The thud of the nightclub beneath your feet
Spiced rum coating teeth
Let you live a life.

The shorts of this playsuit are short-short
For thighs that rub and glide against each other
For freckles to shimmer under
Like constellations
Like a map

To a place you've never been before
But where you'd like to stay.

A body to be seen
Not hidden
To be savoured
In a fitted red playsuit.
Which Clea holds in her hands,
And carries to the changing room.
Where a girl, the warden of the changing room,
Hands over a plastic number one,
with a look in her eyes,
a glare,
at Clea.
Clea who refers to herself as fat because she is,
As a matter of fact
And she loves that.
And really – *it's her body* – so that should be that.

But people make it a problem frequently
Sometimes cruelly
Sometimes patronisingly
Almost daily.

When people review the plays she's in,
They often have more to say about her body than the acting.

'The curvy lead actress, though gifted in comedy timing, isn't
believable as the romantic heroine.'

And now there's That Girl, in charge of the ins and outs of the changing room,
That Girl with that look in her eyes.
Who Clea wouldn't know how to describe, wouldn't be able to pick out from a line,
not because Clea is dismissive but because she's not the kind to scrutinise.

That Girl with whom Clea will spend such a small, miniscule, teeny tiny, amount of time with?

Yes. It is That Girl.

Who, when Clea pulls the curtain back completely unselfconsciously (because why would she be?)
To see herself in the normal distance of the bigger mirror so as to get a bigger picture of her bigger self.

That Girl.

Who, from nowhere, clutching empty hangers, turns and says,

'I think you're a bit too big for that jumpsuit.'

'You think what, sorry?'

And then she says it again.

Clea hears the sound of someone else shuffling in the changing room and then sees a woman pull back her own curtain to spy on the altercation. The woman moves awkwardly, almost as though on Clea's behalf while simultaneously and unsubtly hoping for drama to unfold.

Clea calmly returns to the changing room, not to cry silently, but to take a long look at herself.

She smooths her hands over the playsuit
Relishes how it holds her flesh
The squidge of her back
The round of her belly
She rotates her body in cursive
And watches how the material dances over her skin
Instead of shying from the mirrors she takes it as an honour to see herself at every angle like this.
A body with which she's finally comfortable
In which she can breathe
In which she can live
And it's true her breasts are small
And her belly big
It's true she doesn't fit the socially acceptable hourglass
But it's also true that time is ticking
And she is done with wasting seconds.

She tried to change it too much more than once
Misplaced some of her mind in the process
And her monthly cycle too

Tried the teas

The diets
The stopping
The starting
The counting
The steps
The mess
The knees cold on the bathroom floor

It culminated in the summer she was a bridesmaid for her cousin.
Clea kept telling the dressmaker
'Don't worry don't worry it will fit, I will make sure it fits.'
As though, if it didn't fit, terrible things would happen.
Like the wedding would probably be ruined.
All Clea needed to do was be slim,
She was ashamed of herself for failing in this.

The dressmaker with the tape measure around her neck abruptly
stopped and said:
'Why on earth would you worry about that? We can always get
more fabric.'

From behind her huge glasses,
She looked at Clea
Tailors chalk between her teeth
And saw so many repeated histories.
Memories of women's waists so many times held between her hands
And the new trends forever walking through her door,
Before walking back out again
Always leaving women, for one reason or another, uncomfortable

in their skin
Waist trainers, bum padding, crushingly tight pants
And what was it all for?
She looked up at Clea from the hem of the dress and said,

'There's always a little more calico, cotton and silk.
But you won't get these years back.
You won't get the time you wasted hating yourself back.
You won't even get the knees you currently have.
And definitely not the tits.'

And this changed Clea.

So here she is now,
The lost parts of her mind finally re-found.
Neither her fattest nor her thinnest
But content.
Happy whatever change might come.
Because she's learnt:
That is what a woman is – a body forever in flux.
Subject to change.
Object to no one.
She's learnt:
You either loathe yourself to pieces
Or accept yourself until you know what peace is.
Self-care requires love,
Will not happen from hate.
You can't punish a body into shape
But you can nourish it anywhere
And everywhere

And you should.

Clea whips the playsuit off, gathers her stuff and goes to That Girl.
That Girl holds both hands out, one hand ready for the plastic
number and the other hungry to rip the playsuit back from Clea.

'Oh yeah, no, I'm keeping that,' states Clea.

'Really?' That Girl asks as Clea departs.

Not satisfied, the girl says with snark:

'Well, you do you.'
Clea pauses for a beat,
Considers turning back,
Instead says to herself:

Dimpled thighs
  soft belly
      chubby arms
      cellulite:
        the surface of the moon
  weight:
  that rises,
  falls like the sun
      chins that roll
      like tummies
    some of us are made like this
    and that's lovely.
thick hair

from head to toe
abs flat enough to eat off
slim hips
legs long
articulate
as the
ticks of
a clock
A cups
to
Z cups
some of us
are made
like this
and that's
lovely
deep scars
stretch marks
skin that won't behave
backs that ache
boobs that sweat
nipples that chafe
nipples that feed
elbows of sandpaper
some of us are made like
pears
cucumbers
kiwi
a fresh Cornish brie
a grain of barley

some of us are
a fusion of both
an orange
on a pair of sticks
two beetroots
on two aubergines.
What do you get when
you put us all together?
A feast.

So 'I will' she thinks 'I will, always, do me'
Without looking back.

That night Clea takes the red playsuit for its first spin,
Red as in post box,
As in a love letter to herself.
When she gets home, she runs the shower hot.
Cascading water washes the day off.
Massages cleanser into her skin.
Moisturises deeply.
Drops her towel and grabs her phone.
She takes photo after photo.
For no one, but herself.
Saves them in a hidden folder, which week by week documents the
body she adores.

And when she lays her head on her pillow that night, she makes one
last wish before she sleeps:

I hope That Girl learns to love herself too.

Dil Was Born on a Saturday Afternoon

in the utility room.

On one of those days where the sky is white with clouds, no glimmer of blue, no shard of sun and only memory of moon.

Her big sister, a full sixteen years older, looked at the hairy newborn thing before her, then out of the window and back down again.

Mostly tenderly, but a touch bossily, in that way older sisters innately are, and whispered,

'Go paint your canvas, baby girl,' into Dil's little ear.

Their mum always remarks how everything about Dil was a surprise.

'Dil practically strode out of her womb and into our lives: a couple weeks early, and of course in the room where all the freshly laundered towels were already waiting – like she'd planned it – and of course, of course, of course on a Saturday! Our baby ruled by

Saturn, God of Sowing Seeds!'
(The whole family, a tapestry of mixed Mediterranean ancestry, keenly adore their mythology.)

And it's true:
Dil is a woman of high ambition and Dil is always on a mission.

She's currently 33 and on year three of a five-year plan.
This means she's the Maître d' of a restaurant in one of those grand and gorgeous London hotels.
Dil worked her way up. Worked hard and patiently until she could swap shifts serving bubble and squeak amidst the grease of her local caff for flutes of bubbly in posh hotels.
She loves the hotel, but she hates it too: the bosses, and the way the snootier clientele treats her beloved team, often leaves her asking, 'Does it have to be like this?'
One day, when she has her own establishment, she plans to prove that it doesn't. So she turns up day in, and day out, to gain experience.

At least now it's Christmas. So even though she's exhausted, even though her big sister keeps reiterating, 'Babes you look creamcrackered,' she cherishes these weeks where people visit less for business, more for pleasure.

The hotel guests arrive for a few nights, with high hopes of the magic snow-globe London they've seen in films and Dil works hard to meet those expectations.
The other punters, the ones here for office Christmas dos, indulge hard on the company card. Occasionally, two (sometimes three) of

the Office Christmas Doers, will drunkenly stumble to reception and inquire about the cost of spending a night, so they can really have a good time. On hearing the price, they always change their mind

and jump into taxis

back to their husbands and wives.

So Dil always gets in a little earlier just in case there's anything to catch up on. She's a professional but her intrigue never ceases to be ignited by how many people choose this hotel to house their infidelities.

Last night's team don't have much to report though,

(which is probably good for Dil's growing cynicism).

She heads off to the staff bathrooms to get ready.

She slips off the rose quartz bracelet her best friend gave her (because jewellery is not regulation) and pulls her sleeves over her tattoos (also not regulation).

Spritzes wrists with jasmine scent and

– lividly –

pulls on the unflattering pair of black trousers she mistakenly grabbed this morning.

They're bobbled between the thighs and, ugh, flared

(she is a tapered leg person).

Nonetheless, she still posts a full body mirror selfie with the caption 'Appalling 90's bootcut but ass still fantastic.'

She knows someone will reply saying,

'Girl??? Who you thirst trapping????'

And she'll reply, 'Absolutely no one'

which is true.

Men irritate Dil.

Especially their inability to deliver what they promise.

To Dil, men mean dissatisfaction.

But she does get a kick out of a righteous flirt, so why shouldn't she occasionally entertain someone for a while?

(Even if she will inevitably get bored when they can't keep up.)

She's learnt to stop striking up banter with random men in front of her mother though,

who will excitedly query,

'Ohhh, he seemed nice, did you get his number?' as she envisions grandchildren playing in the heathers.

Dil always bats her enthusiasm down.

'Nah. . . no real chemistry. . . No actual connection! I'd rather win alone than let some man attempt to run rings around me, Mum!'

Of course, wise words from her little Saturn baby.

Her mum always feels the conflict between being terrified Dil might end up alone and extremely impressed by the fact Dil is completely fine with that.

Currently, Dil sucks a mint and assesses the 5 p.m. vibe with her wide eyes. She's happy to see espresso martinis effusively toasted – she'd fought hard to have them included in the Christmas menu. A naughty drizzle of Baileys to make them extra seasonal.

As Dil reminds each waitress to tuck in shirts and smooth skirts, memories of school uniform checks always shoot through her mind. Once a week she'd stand in the blazer her (much taller) sister had passed down and brace herself for whatever creative ridicule the prefects would surely hurl. She won't leave anyone feeling inadequate on her watch now, so she's a force in how she protects her team from the judgement of, not just the staff superiors but the superiority that typifies their clientele.

Dil makes sure everyone is pristine.

Her love is sometimes tough.

But it's genuine.

And it's definitely appreciated.

Her favourite part of her daily ritual is the few minutes she spends with the chefs at the gleaming open kitchen which forms the centrepiece of the space.

She loves to admire their expertise,

arms moving at the speed of light,

Tonight's special is gnocchi.

The certainty of food prep relaxes Dil: throw potato into water and it will boil, no surprises.

Before she can sink into that thought Dil feels a frantic tap on her shoulder. 'Dil, we need to do a swap!'

The head barman has called in sick and, seeing as Dil is the only one around tonight who can mix a cocktail as well as he can (it was her that taught him) she now needs to replace him.

At least no one will see her crap trousers, she thinks, and anyway she's missed being on the bar.

At least the bar faces the rest of the restaurant so she can still keep an eye, she tells herself, as she crosses her fingers and wishes them all a good night.

Once she's checked all the ingredients are stocked and ready to go Dil props her elbows on the bar and admires the enormous Christmas decorations.

Fir tree garlands festoon the ceiling,

woven through with differently sized red and gold baubles.

Fairy lights adorning everything in an enchanting

(but, somehow still tasteful)

glooow.

Just as she's making a mental note to email the designer with praise

in the morning, a man comes in.

Confident as anything.

All the eyes in Dil stop to look at him.

The instant pheromone thrill is dizzying, new in her skin, but she

welcomes it

– because my God, he's buff. So buff.

She knows her niece would make fun of her old-arse slang.

But he is.

And it is what it is.

Braids frame his firm smooth jaw.

And gosh even the way the Christmas lights glimmer against his

nose ring is. . . wow.

She wonders if he's one of the famous men that regularly walks

through these doors, but when she checks the space around him,

she doesn't see an entourage or security.

So, he's ordinary, she thinks, but, like, extraordinary.

And now he's coming towards her.

She holds her breath with no idea whether she's smiling, or rest-

ing-bitch-facing.

In three, two, one

He's facing her now.

She's wrapped up in his aura now.

Taking in his outfit now.

Looking at him looking at her now.

As she parts her lips to greet him, he leans forward and takes a cocktail menu,

she breathes in his aftershave:

mmmmmandarin and sandalwood

The thought streaks across her mind:

Yes,

yes, I absolutely would.

It'll be nice, she thinks, to kick off the evening with a chirpse and flirtation.

He looks up from the menu and flashes her a smile before ordering an Old Fashioned.

Great choice of drink, she thinks.

She feels his eyes on her fresh cherry manicure as she reaches for

sugars,

bitters,

spirit,

ice.

Glad she waited 45 minutes to be seen by Chelsea, specifically, in the nail bar this morning.

Dil meets his eyes as she gently twists the orange peel and drops it into the glass as a final flourish.

As he takes a sip, she waits for him to say how exceptional it is.

He says nothing.

And then,

'I think I'll be using my tab tonight after all. . . it's under "Gard". . .'
Of course he's got a tab she thinks. She wants to find out if he's as
predictable as all the other handsome men she's known before.
She wants to know if, like them, he moves through the world never
giving too much away, just a taste. She wants to know if he believes
women are putty in his hands, either way.
Almost on cue, a waitress bubbles up towards him and asks, 'Can
I take your coat',
Dil assumes work mode, and looks as if to say,
'We both know that is literally not your job'
but the waitress looks back as if to say,
'Can't blame a girl for trying, you're simping just as much as I am.'
Which is true. So Dil breaks away from them both and scans the
bar for empties.
But soon finds herself unable to resist the desire to see what he's
up to now,
Throws a surreptitious glance towards him.
To her surprise he's chasing the same waitress halfway up the floor
waving the notepad she dropped.
Oh God, she realises, he's sweet.
At this moment, Dil can't imagine fancying a total stranger more.

When a woman appears and asks for a white wine that isn't too
sweet but also not too acidic Dil could hug her, thankful to have
something to focus on.
Dil considers the request then pours a small measure of wine for
her to try,
after a quick sip she immediately and zealously approves Dil's
choice.
The whole time Dil feels Gard's eyes on her.

She likes the feel of his attention, so she takes extra time
Let him wait.
Let him wait.

She is good at her job, so when she notices his tumbler already empty, it would be remiss of her not to ask, 'Same again, sir?'
He nods.
'Definitely! Credit where credit's due, you make an excellent drink.'
'Uhuh, I know,' she says.
She watches him note the confidence in her, she feels it reel him closer.
She'd like to sit in this moment a little longer but one of the floor staff is beckoning her over.
She passes him his drink, and goes to save whatever the situation is.

Of course, the problem is mediocre. A mix-up with the booking system. Someone important is on their way in but a table isn't ready.
Dil looks at the floor plan, does the mental arithmetic, and suggests a re-shuffle which puts everything back in perfect order.
They're impressed: she's usually a speedy problem solver but this was double time.
To Dil, though it's felt like far, far longer.
When she gets back to the bar, she's relieved:
Gard is still sitting there.
'Busy day?', he asks,
and with that they get talking.
He's been with a few of the other office-less DJs he knows, an impromptu Christmas session (she forgives his use of the word 'session' because at least when DJs say it it's kind of cool)

'Who knew musicians were craving something so routine?' he jokes.

He asks it with an agenda which Dil ignores in favour of her own.
She needs to know (judge) which bar he's already been to tonight.
She knows the exact one he mentions.
Of course, thinks Dil, of course he likes that one with the exposed
brick work and the projections of fire (he's making the fuckboy
Bingo she's playing with him too easy),
and yet, she can't help but dreamily wonder if he has any tattoos,
what he would think of hers.
She wants to ask what month he was born,
what his star sign is

She asks what he got as his Secret Santa gift.
He plonks a mini Magic 8 ball on the counter.
'Which is a bit pass-aggs I think. My friends are always accusing
me of being flaky'
'Right,' she says.
'Anyway. Do you want to play?'
So now, Dil takes a look around, is pleased everything is ticking
along okay.
Drinks are being sipped and meals tucked into.
'Okay, but ladies first.'
'Always,' he says,
his fingers touching hers ever so briefly as she cheekily grabs the
ball.
She shakes it, torn between asking something funny or something
sexy.

Before she makes her decision a man barks aggressively at her from the other side of the bar.

'Vodka on the rocks, love!'

Both Dil and Gard wait, redundantly, for him to say please.
Dil pours the drink and extends the card machine towards him,
but he fumes, 'I've got a tab. Charge it to the room.' He finishes
the drink in one greedy swig and slams the glass down. Something
about the way he discards the glass reminds her of her own dispos-
ability in the shiny walls of this big hotel. Ten minutes ago she felt
powerful stood behind that bar, now she feels caged in by it.

She would never utter it out loud but sometimes, just sometimes,
Dil is tired of having to work so hard and sometimes, just sometimes
she wonders if the five-year plan is a good one.

As the man starts to walk away, Gard quips at him, 'A thank you
wouldn't kill you, mate.' The man huffs, turns around and sarcasti-
cally, says, 'Thank you so much,' with a glare at Dil which reiterates
his belief that she is, indeed, nothing.

Dil flinches and turns her attention back to Gard:

'I didn't need you to be my knight in shining armour, I just needed
the moment to be over.'

Gard, recognising he's made the situation worse, softens his gaze
apologetically.
And then with question marks in his eyes and more hushed than
before

as though it might be a secret, says,
'Can I ask your name?'
Dil lets an ellipsis pass between them before stating, 'You can.'
After another pause she tells him.
'Dil.' He returns it to her so softly.
Like he's said it a thousand times before,
like he'll say it a thousand times more.

Just as the silence wraps around them both, Dil breaks it. She finds
a reason to run off to the store cupboard, where she stares at all the
ingredients for a second, desperate to find a reason to have dived
in there. She opens the fridge,
lets the cool air hit her,
reminds herself she is at work, and this urge to talk all night to this
man, besides from anything else, is definitely not professional. If the
manager clocks her, she could get in trouble.

But when she comes back out, holding a tray of strawberries in front
of her like a kind of shield he says,
'Dil? That's nice, like the spice?'
She fires back,
'Like the herb. I'd be concerned if you considered dill spicy.'
And he laughs.
An open-mouthed slow *ha ha ha HA* of a laugh.
She needs to make him laugh again and again, she thinks.
The lecture she just gave herself freefalling out the window.

'Another?' she asks, motioning to his second drained glass.
'Please. . . But maybe also some water?'

As she prepares two glasses a troubled look replaces the goofy grin.
In earnest he asks, 'God, is this a terrible place to work?'

With that, a tonne tumbles out of Dil.
Like a passion fruit tipped.
None of her usual walls resist.
A stream of stuff she's heard said.
All the –isms she's heard slip from entitled tongues.
The things her superior has said to her, the efforts to make her feel
small even though she's been here longer than them all.
She talks him through
the presumptions,
patriarchy,
and upheld hierarchy a building like this relies on to make its money.
And all the while he keeps nodding, a safe space for her to put her
information in.
And she feels that, she feels the safety of him.
And it feels good.
Different.
New.

He shakes his head and shakes the Magic 8 ball:
he asks, 'Should Dil leave this job?'

She finds this incredibly presumptuous and wants to say, 'I can't
just leave, there's a plan at play!' but her dreams are her own, not
to be shared with boys she barely knows, so she changes the subject
before the subject even arrives.

'There is one thing I really like about working here at the hotel.'

He signals to her to go on.

'My fave is when girls come in for afternoon tea. . . You know like mothers, and daughters, hen parties. .'

'Yeah. Thank you,' says Gard drily. 'I know what girls are.'
Dil holds back a laugh (because a laugh would draw too much attention to them) and instead steams on, 'So anyway. You know when you can just tell they've saved up for ages to be here? Well . . . I pick some bullshit but very expensive thing and add it to their order.'

He nods and taps the menu. 'Right, yeah. . . like the gold-leaf brownie?'

'Exactly! Exactly like the gold leaf brownie! So when the extra thing comes and just before they panic about getting charged, I say, God sorry, silly me, I got your order wrong! Must have pressed the wrong key! Silly me! And then. . .'

'And then?' he asks on the edge of his bar stool, taking all of Dil in.

'And thennnn. . . I offer them something fizzy as an apology! My chefs call it "the Dil speciality".'
Gard marvels at the simple genius of it before noting,
'Fucking hell, you must be losing this place a packet!'
which Dil immediately waves off.
'These rich fuckers can hack it. Honestly, they're so self-absorbed

they wouldn't notice. Even the owner – when he shows up – is more interested in making eyes at every beautiful woman that glides through the door.'

Gard takes a gulp of whiskey.

He asks,
'God he's not come on to you, has he? The owner? That would be so. . . so. . .'

She shakes her head and watches relief flush through him before he flips back,

'That's really sweet of you to do that, for those girls I mean. . . you don't immediately give off "sweet" as a vibe, but yeah.'
Dil nods 'Yeah, I know. I don't intend to. Sweet? Ugh. Nope, not me.'
(Dil always tells this lie, always upholds this façade amongst strangers.)
She wants to ask what sort of first impression she gives off.
And what his type is.
Instead, she says 'I'll tell you a secret though.'
She watches his attention magnify.
'I've got a deal going with one of the chefs, sometimes he puts back a cake or two for me. I am terrible for sugar. . . That salted caramel thing? Chef's kiss. The Christmas specials? Incredible.'

'Well. . .' he says, 'That's great, that leaves more savoury for me.'

She wants to ask what his takeaway of choice would be on a cosy night in

and what foods he hated as a child but loves now.

Instead she wipes the bar and checks when the next reservation is due.

But he's not letting it go, and with a directness he asks, 'So. You got someone to cook you dinner?'

'Not tonight' she says, without looking up from the screen.

And then she turns the table on him. 'What about you, no woman to cook for the DJ?'

He hesitates before saying, 'There was until very recently. Fun vibes only right now. Nothing serious.'

'Uhuh,' she says, not exactly sure herself of what the uhuh means (for either of them).

As she's planning her next move (should she ask a question or should she make a statement) she notices the owner walk in and immediately straightens her back. She doesn't like him, but all promotions lie in his hands. Gard notices the immediate shift in her energy and turns around to find out what she's looking at.

'The chief Dick,' she whispers to Gard as they both watch him stride in and acknowledge a few of the regulars.

As he walks over Dil prepares for the usual brief grilling and curt tone. But then, before her eyes, he pats Gard on the shoulder and says,

'Hello hello! Sorry I'm late, I hope you haven't had too many? Why didn't you go straight to the table? You could have got a starter? Some of those lovely olives? I don't pay the bar staff to be distracted by you, you know?'

This almost makes Dil laugh, because of course she's so inter-changeable to him that he doesn't realise she's one of his senior managers. But then her eyes come back to Gard who coolly says, 'Hey Dad. Firstly, I don't like olives. And secondly—'

The boss cuts Gard off. 'Alright, alright. No olives! Let's get to the table, I'm starving.'

Dil has two thoughts.

She, too, doesn't like olives, and: 'Dad'. . . Did he say 'Dad'?

The Boss has already started making his way to the table, but Gard is slowly and deliberately gathering his coat. He waits for Dil to say something, sensing he should take her lead.

But Dil, who has never considered what it might feel like to *be* gobsmacked, is currently finding out.

She watches as he tears himself away and follows his father. The second he's gone, the waitress from earlier rushes over and says, 'Oh fuck! Didn't you know?!'

The bar gets louder as more and more people pile in, so Dil does what Dil does best: she powers through her shift. For a while that works, for a while she's distracted enough. Until a little lady comes in – small enough that she can just about see above the counter and says,

'Ooh, someone seems to have left their things. . . I'll give you that. . . and can I have. . . hmm. . . I think a glass of the house red?'

As Dil looks at the items, the alarm she set herself earlier goes off, reminding her she's due a break. She shoves them in her pocket, serves the lady and races outside.

As soon as she takes in her first breath of fresh air in hours, it starts to rain.
Thank fuck, she thinks.
Feeling her body unwind.
She rolls her sleeves up so the breeze can get into her skin.
She loves the rain.
The feeling of everything being washed away, the sky clearing. making way for change,
for wide open blankness: that feeling that anything could happen, that she can make anything happen.
She always takes the rain as a sign. What the sign is, leaves her uncertain tonight.
She can't remember which planets are retrograding and which are stationing.
But she can feel them moving.

Maybe she's been watching too much romantic comedy, she thinks, because obviously, he wasn't really interested in me. He's probably laughing with his dad – at my expense.

'And even if he was interested, do I even have time?' She asks herself.
With that she comes back to herself.
Remembers herself.
Soothes herself.
His loss, she says to herself, his loss.
And she means this.

Even if he did make her feel seen.
Even if he did make her feel heard.
Even if he did make her feel like she could be herself.

As she opens the door ready to return to the grind,
he walks through it.
'Hey' he says.
'Hey. . . coincidence! I was just about to come and find you.' She
reaches into her pockets and extends the items to him.
'I don't believe in coincidence,' he smiles.
Dil is taken aback ever so slightly, because neither does she.
'But. . . in fairness. . . I have been watching you for an hour waiting
for you to have a break.'
They share a glance at the words still shining on the face of the 8
ball between them:
'Cannot Predict Now'
She holds it as carefully as she holds her mother's healing crystals.
As Gard takes the ball back, he taps the room key in her palm and
says:

'I left that. . . on purpose. . . for you. Maybe. . . see you later, Dil?'

She looks at him curiously and he looks not at but into her.
The tinny ring of her alarm goes off, beckoning her back inside.
She slides the key into her pocket and leaves him in the open door.

Later, when the restaurant is finally closed and the Christmas
cracker hats and riddles have been scooped away, she takes longer
to change back into her jeans than everyone else.

She lingers in the mirror longer than she usually does.
She takes out the key and allows herself to look at it.
To consider the possibility.
Room 111.
Of course.
Angel numbers.
What are the chances of that she thinks
Her wrist feels better with her bracelet back on.
But she doesn't feel quite herself.

She looks at the key again.
Contemplates what she'll do next.
She remembers, certain as Saturn, anything can happen,
Certain as Saturn *she* can make anything happen.

Rey Walks into
a Hair Salon

And says she needs something new.

'Oooh exciting! A whole new look?' enquires Lainey, the hairdresser.
'A whole new life,'

comes the reply without a pause,
words absent-mindedly released,
words in the ether now as sounds,
words that were meant to stay as thoughts.

Rey attempts to put the words back, 'Sorry! Overshare. . .'

But Rey feels lighter for taking the words out of her chest and placing them there, at the hands of this woman. This Lainey of 'Lainey's

Ladies', the salon Taffy has recommended to Rey. Rey had liked
her bubbly tone on the phone, now in person she's even more like
a glass of prosecco in human form.

'Oh! Don't worry, I've been doing hair since I was eighteen'
She gestures to the gold balloons emblazoned with curly pink letters
which read 'Happy Anniversary'.
'It's only my first year as salon owner, I've been doing hair for far,
far longer. Trust me, I've heard it all before.'

Lainey has – she's heard harsher,
And darker and worse.

Lainey also knows better than to meet an embarrassed Rey's gaze.
Lainey doesn't need to make Rey feel stared at, observed, uncomfortable, or judged, so she doesn't. Instead, Lainey checks the clock,
and slides her hand down the appointment book to 4 p.m.
'Ah yesss,' she says remembering their lengthy phone consultation.
Rey's unease, though quiet, had buzzed incessantly as she asked
several questions. Anyone else might have heard a tricky customer
nitpicking, but Lainey knows it well: the way self doubt creeps into
a life and takes control, makes even small interactions irritable,
tense, flavoured with cortisol.

'Rey. Beautiful name. You're a bit early. Coffee while you wait?'
Rey says yes, then no, then yes, then no again.
Lainey just keeps drawing the dots between the cloaked panic of the
phone call and the decision that can't be made now.
'Or we have herbal teas? Peppermint? That'll match your jumper!
Rey nods, barely aware what she'd chucked on before leaving.

She's been sorting through her mum's house today.
Shredding hospital letters,
Playing with the perfumes on her mum's dresser.

Lainey watches Rey – the picture of so many things Lainey has seen and seen. And been and been.

Lainey suggests Rey looks online for 'hairspiration' but Rey struggles to do so because the images of well-put-together girls don't speak to her. For distraction, she reaches for the paperback, but she still can't get into this book Mel has insisted she read. She decides to watch Lainey work, grateful for the relentless white noise of the hairdryer that dulls the noise in her head.
When it's Rey's turn, the way the pink gown causes her to blend into the pastel landscape of the salon pleases her.
'So. Welcome to Lainey's Ladies!'
'Thank you, it's so. . . err. . .pink?'
It is, in fact, more shades of pink than Lainey (and even Rey with all her vocabulary) knows how to name.

'Yeah, growing up I was always in my brother's hand-me-downs so as soon as I got the chance, I've been like 'Give me fuchsia! Give me baby pink!' Hahaha. Anyway, what are we doing today?'
 And all Rey can say is: 'It's all a bit of a mess.'
Lainey jokes that mess is her speciality, that her regulars say it's as though she was born holding a comb. Ready to untangle a mess. Any mess.
And today will not be an exception, thinks Rey.

Lainey runs a paddle brush through the patchwork quilt of unevenly dyed hair and says,

'Hmm, so a few different things seem to have happened here.'

The obviousness of the statement actually makes Rey laugh:

'Err so I went dark, then wanted to go lighter, so I got a stripper kit and then it went a bit, err. . .'

'Ginger?'

'Yeah, ginger. So. . .'

'So you dyed it. . . even. . . darker?'

'Yep.'

'Right. Why did you go darker still then?'

'Well, the first time was an accident, I was just like. . . like. . . not concentrating in the shop, grabbed the nearest box, didn't realise it would be so. . .'

'It's no biggy. We can break it up with hmmm. . . maybe something like this? Oh and a few streaks of this. . . oh yeah that really suits you. What do you think? Layers around your face?'

Rey looks at the swatches of colour, trying to decipher meaning from them, trying to gain a sense of who she'll be in a few hours' time. The truth is she kept changing her hair because a part of her really did believe new hair would mean new life.

Lainey looks into the hair and says 'full restyle' the way a magician might say abracadabra.

Not because she really cares about the answer, but because she just feels she should say something – Rey asks how long it will all take: 'I'll do my best to get it done in good time.'

'No honestly, I'd rather you didn't rush. Take your time. I'm good.'

Lainey lets the words go over her head – people always say things like 'take your time' to their hairdressers when really, it's not just about the time Lainey might take. It's also about the bleach, the heat, the speed of chemical reactions.

In that way that nice women tend to, Lainey chits and chats. As she does so Rey notices the dazzling glint of amber in her hazel eyes. Rey's mum had always told her, 'Look people in the eye', and now, Rey can see why.

Just as Rey sinks into the rhythm of the comb weaving through her hair, a shrill phone ring pierces through the room. Lainey rushes to the reception desk to take the call saying,

> 'This is why I'm desperate for another pair of hands! And sorry by the way, I know that's a really loud ring, but it has to be so I can hear it over the hairdryers, innit?'

Rey suppresses the urge to investigate the packets of foil in her hair. A part of her wants to unfold them, wants to know what's happening inside. When Lainey returns, Rey asks her how she got into hairdressing. Rey asks because she likes the quality of Lainey's speech: it oscillates between sing-songy buoyancy and then punchier, more professional moments. Lainey obliges the question and Rey is glad of that.

Fifteen years ago, Lainey was doing an admin job up town. She hated the job but her family (her mum, her dad, the four brothers she was the centrepiece of) needed the money, so she had to pull her weight, back and forth to work every day. On the bus in, she watched a loop of the same people get on and off. It wasn't long before she'd acquired an internal photo album.

There were: three teenagers with identical side fringes and a zeal for straighteners. They'd gossip until the one who lived at stop three alighted, at which stage the remaining two would mock every word she'd just said. Lainey was sure there must be a reason because, otherwise she couldn't understand why women would be so cruel without justification.

There was also: a few times a week, a couple in their twenties who would stumble on at stop six, seemingly, to kiss and kiss and kiss, his dreads resting on her collar, her loose curls grazing shoulder blades. Their romance always sweeping Lainey up.

There was also: the woman at stop nine with a short blunt salt-and-pepper bob who always took too long to gather the loose change required for the fare. Lainey was always ready with her open purse.

But mostly: there was the lady, smoothed caramel streaks and middle parting, who owned the salon opposite the bus stop itself. Forever sweeping.

Most days Lainey would see the shutters hoisted up in the morning and back down in the evening. The hairdresser worked more hours than most but was always smiling, always passionately committed to whatever she was creating. Lainey wanted that, the joy of a space which felt like her sanctuary and the satisfaction of transformations forever poised in her fingertips.

Lainey's fascination built and built until finally – held firm in her belief that if you don't ask you don't get – after a convenient half day, she fizzed through the door and said,

> 'Ok hear me out: I can't afford to pay, buuut I've noticed it's just you. . . so maybe you could do my hair like the lady in the window and in return I could be your Saturday girl for the day?'

The hairdresser looked her up and down. The soles of Lainey's shoes worn thin, the hood of a boy's coat hanging by a thread, scraggy split ends.

It took Lainey one afternoon to prove she was good enough to learn the trade.

Fifteen years later, a 'for sale' sign went up by the door and her boss tired now, ears hard of hearing after years of hairdryers blasting now, and wrists stiffer now gestured to the sign and said

'Lainey, it's yours – if you want it?' I've spoken to your brothers and they're all chipping in. It's your turn now my love. You'll be great. Buy that foot spa I told you about, okay?'

'And the rest is history I guess?' She says to Rey as she looks around the pink paradise.

'That's a really lovely story,' says Rey.

Rey likes Lainey, feels drawn to her, feels comfortable with her, but just as Rey readies another question the phone rings again. Lainey pootles off to get it. When she comes back her tone isn't joyful or light. Her face is a pale, panicked white.

'Shit, I'm so sorry, but I need to go, my niece just got knocked off her bike and I need to go and. . .'

'Oh my god, is she ok?'

'I don't know. That was the nurse – said she's fine, broken leg but that's it.'

'Well that's good!'

'It is, isn't it? It's ok, isn't it? It could have been worse, couldn't it?'

'It is, it is. Take a deep breath, it's alright.'

'My brother will kill her if he finds out she's been bunking college, kill us both if he finds out I knew, Aunt Lainey to the rescue and on the block again.'

That makes sense to Rey: Lainey the rebel aunt you can go to.

Rey has the feeling Lainey is the kind of woman you could call at 4 a.m. and say you need a morning-after pill or guidance on re-wiring a plug. There's a sense that whatever a person could need she'd be able to give it. She has the eyes of someone who has de-escalated a thousand people a thousand times.

And yet right now she's on the edge and Rey recognises herself in her. Rey rises, foils rustling and cape swishing. Heads to the kettle and carefully but quickly, pours out a fresh chamomile tea, topping the boiled water with a little cold so Lainey won't burn her mouth.

'Just sip,' says Rey. 'Just sip and sip until the feeling washes away,' says Rey.

Rey remembers an article she read recently about how the heart has a magnetic field around it. She considers the fact she's been in Lainey's heart space all afternoon, and Lainey in hers.

Rey knows what it means to answer that one call which changes you. She knows the way a hand will struggle to grip the phone. The way your whole world comes unspun. And the battle to focus, to absorb all and any information. But she also knows this situation is different from her own. The niece is fine, alive. Rey needs to get out of her own head and help Lainey. So thinks and then she instructs:

'We should breathe.'

Lainey nods as Rey takes the lead,

'Breathe in for four. Hold it for four. And out for four. Okay and again.'

Following Rey's count, Lainey breathes and breathes and breathes. Lainey breathes until she knows things will be fine. In and out, in and out until she can say,

'God sorry, what am I like?! What an overreaction. I'm so sorry!' Without words, they instinctively conspire to pretend the situation is funny.

*

The next afternoon Rey is back in the salon again, ready to finish the appointment that got cut short yesterday.
'Lucky I'd managed to do the colour, that would have been a 'mare!' Expecting a nod of agreement, but receiving nothing, Lainey remembers that Rey patently knows nothing about hair. But Rey does know how to calm a storm.

'Thank you so much for yesterday Rey, it really helped.'

'Oh, come on, don't be silly, I barely did anything.'

'But that's exactly it, it was so simple, so calming, honestly, you're amazing. I now know exactly who to call in a crisis.'

'It's what anyone would do.'

'It really isn't. Honestly, thank you.'

When Lainey does people's hair, and she can sense they're troubled or that there's something wrong she says mantras in her head for them. With every brush she thinks things like 'I hope you realise how loved you are' or 'I hope you dump your shit fucking boyfriend'. Now as she glides the comb through Rey's hair she says again and again 'I hope you find what you're looking for, Rey.' Sometimes, her nosiness interrupts the flow though.

'We didn't even do the basic chat yesterday – if you've got a boyfriend or not. . .?'

'Oh. I'm single!'

'Ready to mingle?'

'Why? Are you setting up an in-salon dating agency?'

Lainey titters, she knows it's silly, but she loves the idea of being matchmaker. She also feels the pensive shift in Rey though, remembers all the times others have said the same sorts of things to her. The love lives of single women in their thirties so often treated as matters of public enquiry after all. Treated as a problem to be solved. She knows how sometimes, even if well intentioned, other people's romantic advice can feel trite, bordering on unkind, sometimes quite cruel. She cheerfully drops the topic and embarks on a commentary of the weather instead. To her surprise, after a while,

Rey says after a deep breath,

> 'This isn't a post-break-up haircut. It's a homecoming haircut. I was with someone for a while, but that's not why I'm here, not really. I lost my mum, and her house is round the corner, I moved back a little while ago. I've been putting this off for ages, if I'm honest. Don't totally know why. Mum always loved getting her hair done though . . . I'm just trying to come home. Return to myself.'

Lainey's hands haven't stopped gliding the scissors through Rey's hair and she knows this is part of the specific alchemy which allows people to tell their hairdressers things they wouldn't tell others. Her niece, who's doing Drama A-Level (when she turns up to school), says it's because there's a fourth wall, like in the theatre. Lainey agrees, remembers sitting in this same chair so many years before, her own trauma tumbling out of her: debt and needs unmet, expressed to the woman who offered her the job she'd always dreamed of. The job that changed and kept changing her life.

Lainey grabs another brush – Rey really does have a lot of hair – and ponders what the best response is. Here's when the door is shoved open by a crutch. A young woman hobbles in.
'Hello auntiiiieeeeee'
Lainey greets her niece.

Rey gasps. She looks like the girl in a photograph on her mum's fridge, same exact expression and everything. The girl in the photo is Rey, aged eighteen, when her whole life was ahead of her. Seeing this carbon copy of herself makes Rey want to shield the niece from all the ways her days could drastically change.

Rey watches the niece in the mirror. Her unruly hair taking up the background, herself in the foreground and Lainey in the middle. She misses the young woman she never got to be. That girl in the photograph on the fridge.

Her mum loved that photo.

Lainey watches her tip jar get raided and notices the way Rey seems taken aback. Her eyes flit between the two. She sees it too.

The familiarity Lainey and Rey feel making sense to them both.

As the pair of crutches hobbles out and to the shop Rey wishes, really wishes this young girl well.

When the hair is done, Lainey dances hairspray through the air, it's sweet scent floats through the room, almost cloying but not quite. Lainey shows Rey the back, the perfect circles of blow-dried curls springing up under her touch. Lainey looks at Rey with so much affection and so much hope that Rey almost struggles to bear it. Almost wants to look away and avoid it. But she doesn't. She takes a breath, and allows herself to soak it in.

'It really suits you,' says Lainey.

She looks more like her mum now than ever. People have always said it, but she hasn't always seen it. The hair, yes of course, but now she sees the eyes, now she sees the grief. The feeling overwhelms her. But she can't look away either. She is lost for what to say. So she doesn't say anything. Just feels the usual burning in her chest, the never-ending sensation of wanting to cry but never being able to.

'A trim every six weeks would be good. If you want to come back of course?'

This is the most at home Rey has felt in months.

'Yes, please' says Rey 'Can I book it in now?

Magenta
Moves In

Ruby loved a market.

Markets were her jam,

where she always spent her bread and butter.

Whenever she moved anywhere new, which was often because

Ruby was one of those people who moved a lot

She would look up what's good, borough by borough,

When she asked new neighbours what the local was like she didn't
mean the pub,

no, what she needed to know was where the stainless steel bowls
gleamed silver,

spilling over with blueberries, blackberries and bananas.

And sometimes, among her neighbours, kindred spirits would reveal
themselves as they trundled past her window laden with goodies,

But mostly, her neighbours would say, 'Oh. . . I have no idea, I do it all online.'

Ruby loved to hear stall holders conduct themselves like a raucous orchestra in the last hour,
'Three for a pound, three for a pound.
Get them now, get them now!'
The thrilling urgency of the last-minute bartering and bargaining.
The satisfaction of the haul.

She loved the reams and reams of fabrics
in all the prints she could imagine,
and some prints she couldn't.
Leaning closer – is that a peacock sipping a cocktail?
Is that a cat reading a book?
All the colours she could fathom
and all the colours in between,
net curtains in not quite white, not quite vanilla.
Sheets and sheets of sequins,
zips and zips and zips,
a crate full of iron on stickers,
their prices scrawled on neon cardboard stars with felt tips.
Miles and miles of tablecloth material,
Not quite fabric and not completely plastic.
Wipe clean
She liked the one printed with clementines,
but hadn't had a dining table in years.
She would look at them longingly,
Comb her fingers through the fringe of her pixie trimmed hair

and say, one day maybe, one day near.

For Ruby, markets were about being where a fiver meant something.
Where she was free to question everything.
She loved this life:
A life always headed to where the sunflowers are sold among the
turmeric and Tupperware.

Whenever she moved, she was never without her bearings for long.
Often, she'd set out and know she was heading in the right direction
by finding herself in the throng,
among couples holding an orchid like it was their newborn daughter,
who'd smile and gesture, 'Yep, just two more corners, we're coming
from there now, look how lovely this is!'
And she'd say, 'Excellent! Excellent find.'
Honouring the code between them,
market goer to market goer,
congratulating that thing you found that's one of a kind.

These places were so much more to Ruby than items in brown
paper,
these places were about humanity,
no matter what chaos, somewhere, always, the men were playing
dominoes
while behind them a stall holder organised the clothes on her rails.

She had an eye for the practical
 and the beautiful
 and the beautifully practical.

Her bathroom was always well organised – soap dishes which
matched the colours of the walls
She had an enthusiasm for texture too.
For fluffy rugs,
and velvet cushion covers she'd stroke as she watched films.
Each new home was a project.
A whole new nest.
So she was forever chasing ephemera,
forever searching for something that reminded her of her grandma,
gold gilt photo frames
or a summer fête she'd been to –
bunting.
And yes, the fish smelt awful,
but even in that there was something enchanting, something
visceral.
And anyway, her nose would somehow always lead her to hot tea
in polystyrene cups.

Her feet always plodded independently beneath her,
calling her towards hidden treasures.

Wicker baskets. Fake feathers. A love affair with tat.
Markets always felt alive, living, breathing.

Unlike, the gallery she's been working in.
Monday, Wednesday, Friday.
There, the polished grey floor slid beneath her platform trainers
The gallery lacked both bargains and bargaining:
No one stood their ground,
no one ever said, 'What if I don't want to move clockwise through

the exhibition room?'
Ruby resented the way her colleagues would herd the gallery goers across the space,
so she made sure to offer the people in her rooms free rein.
Wouldn't even tell them when they got too close to the sensors,
just let the alarm bleat and then watch as they'd jump back,
Sometimes they'd hold up their hands as if to say – I'm sorry! I wasn't going to steal the art!
And Ruby would look down, stifling a laugh.

Her floor manager would storm over admonishingly.
'Why didn't you remind them to step back?' He'd hiss.
'And don't forget to tell them they're not allowed to so much as *sip* a drink.'
'You'll never get promoted if you carry on like this,' motioning to the ordered power indicated by the colours sewn into his lanyard.
The white signified him to be, professionally speaking, her superior.

Sometimes when handing over the audio headsets, she'd mentally recite her own version of the tour

'Take a left at the crap drawing of empty glasses,
      turn a corner and ask yourself what the point of art is,
before you have the chance to decide,
remind yourself that that drawing costs more than the average person makes in a lifetime.'

Despite all this, she adored the job for how it allowed her to people watch.
To see what drew people closer and what didn't.

To her, art was always about the experience rather than the thing itself.

She loved to look at people looking,

she'd thoughtfully watch the conversations people had with each piece.

She had always been interested in this:

The ways art can ask, and the ways art can answer.

The stories it can tell.

It was just a shame that the pieces in this particular gallery tended not to say much at all

Often leaving her empty, and even worse, uninspired.

But there was something quite mesmerising about the forever-smell of fresh paint

which did at least offer her a glimmer of possibility, a sense of change.

One afternoon, after a tense staff meeting, Ruby called her mum, Madge offered approximately zero sympathy and, in fact, said,

> 'Ugh, silly job. I don't know what you expect. You might as well be a librarian, lurking around in silence.'

Ruby, a little surprised by her mum's inexplicable distaste for librarians, pointed out that librarians train and do a great deal more than lurk around.

> 'You're right. That's true! My cousin is a librarian and she's a very educated woman. But she actually wanted to be a librarian.'

Ruby didn't say anything back.

Meanwhile on the other end of the phone Magenta swore she could hear the sound of Ruby shifting her knees the way she always did when she knew her mum was right.

> 'But you do know what I'm saying, Roobs? You know I just think you deserve to actually achieve the things you've always wanted to achieve? You've always wanted a creative life so why are you hiding on the sidelines now?'

Ruby sighed down the phone because yes, she did know what her mum was saying.

Madge couldn't get her head around the gap between the incredibly capable child who would sit happily at her little orange table painting, drawing, collaging until something wonderful was formed – cardboard spaceships and seascapes made of glued down sweet wrappers – to the woman Ruby had now become. A woman who could put her skills to anything, but didn't.

> 'Yeah. . . I know what you're saying, Mum. . . I do. . .'

And Madge took that to be the huge step forward that it was, because for the first time Ruby had acknowledged an understanding of where her mother was coming from. The first building brick, Madge thought, vowing then to guard it with her life.

To outside ears the gaps between their words may have sounded frayed, as strained as the rope that stops the boat disappearing from the shore. Who exactly was the anchor between them had always been up for debate. But Ruby and Madge knew that a good relationship is one where the roles can swap, are free to change, because, after all, we're not always in the midst of our best days. And Madge wanted to learn from Ruby as much as Ruby wanted to learn from Madge.

So Ruby confessed.

'Yeah, I guess I am a little stuck.'
'Oh Ruby,' said Madge in response.

In that way only a mother can pitch an 'oh'.
An 'oh' of love and panic.
An 'oh' that says, 'I love you more than life, but you're not fulfilling your potential and honestly I can't stand it'.

'Right. Ruby. When are you going to get it together?'

And with that Ruby felt attacked, so attacked back with a performed nonchalance bordering on cruel:

'Dunno, Mum. Probably never.'
Before hanging up.

Ugh, thought Madge, regretting being so abrupt – they were doing well, she shouldn't have pushed it. *Typical me, always putting my foot in it.*

Ruby immediately regretted the way she'd just hung up and went to call her mum back, ready to say, 'Look, I know you've got my best interests at heart. . . I'm just working things out. . . I promise,' but she made the excuse to herself that Madge had Pilates soon and she didn't want to make her late.

Moments like this always reminded Ruby of the egg thing. When she was a kid, she'd spent all day decorating eggs for the yearly Easter term competition at school. A competition she'd won almost every year. A lot was resting on that year's entry because next year she'd be off to secondary school. She regarded it as her grand finale. Her parting gift. She'd made a scene which consisted of a family of eggs in a garden. The grandma egg had a soft cotton shampoo and set, the mama egg had hair made from different coloured pipe cleaners and the daddy egg was at the end of the garden. She'd made a pond out of an upturned bottle lid, even filled it with water. She'd placed a row of washing up sponges green side up to act as the grass for the scene, AND to cushion the eggs – she was particularly impressed by her own logic there.

The whole time Madge had been upstairs on the phone.

When she came downstairs Ruby dragged her by the hand to the world she'd created in a shoe box.

'Look! Look what I made, Mum!'

'Well done, sweetheart.'

'What's your favourite bit?'

'Oh. . . err, all of it. . .' said Madge, pushing past to get to the kitchen.

By the time Madge shook off the stress of the phone call and realised she'd been too brusque towards her favourite artist, it was too late. Ruby had smashed every single one of the eggs, filling the box with yolk.

Still reeling at her mum's dismissal, she sat on the stairs, waiting for Magenta to make the discovery.

When her mum finally went into the room, Ruby held her breath and waited to be summoned.
Instead, she heard her mum sob into the family made of broken shells.

Now, very much an adult, holding the phone in her hand having lashed out at Magenta again, Ruby felt that same guilt.

Because the truth was, yes, Madge had got it wrong many, many times:
Ruby turning up at the school disco in fancy dress when it wasn't fancy dress
Ruby always being the last one to be picked up of all the party guests.

But mostly, Madge got it right.

When Ruby would phone, lost, lonely in the middle of the night, Madge would go to her, wherever she was, and bring her home to chamomile and cuddles.
Ruby knew she could tell her mum of any trouble.

But with this gallery thing, they didn't see eye to eye.
Madge couldn't see why her daughter was sat in a corner watching the world go by.
Sometimes Ruby still wonders what the phone call had been on the day of the eggs.

Often she tries to piece together what else her mum had been deal-
ing with,
often still hears the sobs.
Reminded that her mum was her mum,
but also a really young woman
in her twenties with a child about to start secondary school.
More often than not, she looks at her mum with total awe.

Now on Thursdays they meet for lunch
and everyone always presumes they're sisters.
On this particular Thursday, Ruby sat waiting for Magenta who
arrived in a flurry,
surprisingly decisive about what she wanted to eat.
tapping her hand on her knees
Ruby could see that Madge was feeling antsy.

Ruby peered at her mum, melted cheese dripping from her lips
and asked:

'Come on, Mum, spit it out? What's going on?'

Magenta shuffled awkwardly in her seat before confessing,

'I'm struggling to pay my rent.'

Ruby sighed in relief because she'd been expecting something
worse. She made a suggestion,

'Okay. . . so. . . up your hours, maybe? Would that help?'

Which Magenta totally ignored.

'Do you know what I've been thinking about?' asked Madge.
'Go on. . . ?'
'Those gold picture frames in your flat. . .'
'What about them?'

Something about the gold gilt picture frames had saddened Madge.
She knew Ruby only collected them because they reminded them
of her own mum.
And that was definitely sweet. Definitely something Madge understood.
But what Madge needed to hear was why Ruby never actually put
any photos in the frames?

Why her flat was full of stock photography of fake families?

'I guess. . . because when I look at pictures of us, they aren't
always happy memories.'

Madge knew that was the answer that was coming. But it didn't
make it any easier to hear.

Eventually she found the courage to ask the next question on her
mind.

'I was thinking, what if I move in with you?'

'Mum, it's been a long time since we lived together.'

Madge went to take a bite of her panini, stopped just before it reached her lips and responded.

'Yeah, I know, honey. Not since you were a teenager.'

Ruby had left to study History of Art at university.

Madge had packed her off with a hamper of her favourite things.
The sweets she loved,
postcards of cherished places,
the number for every local resource she could possibly need,
a handwritten guide on what to do if you suspect a gas leak.

In her second year of university Ruby made a surprise visit to celebrate her mum's 38th birthday,
She rang the doorbell and held out a giant bouquet.
On seeing her daughter before her,
Madge gasped in total horror,
tears formed in her eyes as she told Ruby she shouldn't have come
Quickly tugging at her sleeves
but not fast enough that the blots of purple weren't seen.
Eyes sleepless,
jaw swollen,
hair thinner.
Ruby's father shouted from the room where he was eating his dinner,
'Who is it?!'
She'd always known her father was a merciless critic and had always feared that one day he'd replace words with fists.

It had slowly simmered for years,
but in the last three come to a boil:
the violence in him
that Madge hadn't seen since they were just kids,
when it's true he'd been a bully.
But she *had* always coaxed out the best in him
until she hadn't,
couldn't anymore.

And now Madge stood there hoping and hoping he wouldn't come
to the door.

'You have to go,' said Madge.
'I can't leave you here with him!'
'You have to go, Roobs. Go. I'll call you tomorrow.'

Madge had never quite understood that phrase 'a problem shared
is a problem halved'.
Instead she believed survival meant dividing herself into parts,
so there was a persona she adopted in the playground and then
another at work.
Madge contained multitudes and she'd always hoped that would
be power enough,
because she refused, from her depths, to drag Ruby into any of this.
For a while, ever hopeful,
she truly thought the storm might pass
but as she stood on their doorstep now,
fearing Ruby's safety, telling her to leave and leave fast,
a white butterfly floated into her view.

And she knew then that it was her mother, Magenta's mother
had come.
Memories of Magenta's upbringing filled the hollows of her stomach.
Worse than any physical punch: the agony of seeing her own mum
in pain at the hands of her father.
It's so true thought Madge: the body remembers what the brain
files away.
And perhaps her own childhood was why she'd accepted it,
felt she had to, felt she should
but also knowing what her own mother would say if she could.
And in a way she was, was saying her piece,
that white butterfly in the doorframe,
arriving with Ruby, just in time for Magenta's 38th birthday.

Madge knew then that being a mother
meant so much more than playing wife,
it was time now, for a whole new life.

Ruby returned to her course but called her mum every night.
They established a secret code they could use on the phone
if it ever went too far,
but Ruby tossed and turned most nights, unsure what 'too far'
really meant.
Madge attended house viewings in secret, scrimped and saved for
future rent.

And on the day it finally happened she didn't think of it as her
leaving him,
but as her, finally arriving.

Since then, Madge has rented a one bed flat above a launderette, which has made her happy.

On weekends the drama students from next door perform plays to an audience of tumble dryers.

Madge would often go down to listen, certain they would soon be cataclysmically famous.

The street, as well, was busy in that way that suburbs of London are With people who knew better than to leave their cars unlocked or bags half open

people who also refuse to eat olives out of a jar.

But really, Madge would have slept under a car if it meant she'd be close to Ruby. Which she was. Ruby popped in throughout the week with biscuits and tea.

> 'But, Mum – you love being on your own?'
> 'I fancy a change. Don't you?'

There was something about the way that Madge suggested it. Something about the timing. Something about the way a different question floated between them both – loud in its unsaidness.

Does Mum want a change, or is Mum trying to change me?

And yet Ruby didn't resist it, because deep down Ruby didn't want change, she wanted the same: the same as everybody else.

There were years she'd missed out on with her mum.
She had been propelled into grown-upness fast.

> 'Go on then yes, let's do it.'

Together they decided to make a whole new nest,
so it wasn't Ruby's place that Madge was crashing,

But ours!

They found a two-bedroom new build, big kitchen, view of the park.

The move-in day took hours, serious hours on account of all Ruby's
accumulated stuff.
Previously Madge's lack of post-divorce belongings had felt
quite pitiful
but now, with a tired back from carrying her daughter's things
upstairs, she felt thankful.
When they paused for coffee, Madge sifted through one of the many
boxes of fabrics.
Ruby readied herself for a lecture
but Madge could see exactly what Ruby's fascination was.

The more they settled into their new world together the more Ruby
realised how much she'd missed out on. Home cooked meals and
excessive lines of questioning.

They cooked with ingredients they didn't understand but had been
highly recommended by the fruit and veg man,
they watched soap operas in all the languages they knew between
them
(and some of the languages they didn't),
they drank gin and tonic from plastic goblets while fingers dipped
into square dishes of peanuts. Every day it felt more and more like
the purest form of love.

As contentment cradled them they started to ease into a confidence
which allowed them to welcome back the joys they'd neglected.
Ruby returned to creating,
Madge to dating.

In the spirit of so much changing and feeling braver than ever, Ruby
applied for a new job – which she described to Madge, on the way
home after the interview without taking even one breath:

> 'Oh god, Mum, it's an incredible job in an incredible
> gallery. I hope I get this; I really hope I do. And there will
> even be artistic opportunities if I do. Space! To show some
> of my own work! And I'd have a say in the programming of
> other artists too. No more just watching, NOT that I didn't
> genuinely love the watching – before you start – but it's my
> dream job, Mum. Oh god. What if I don't get it?'

> 'You will, Ruby. You will. I've got a really good feeling!'

And it turned out to be true that sometimes mother knows best.

And with the money from the pay rise, Ruby was able to invest
in herself,
in an easel
and a dressmaker's mannequin.

And while all the ideas that had for too long been fighting for attention in Ruby's mind were slowly
beginning to be heard,

night after night Madge stomped from closet to kitchen asking Ruby which date outfit she preferred.

And Ruby was largely unhelpful, because what Madge felt about mortgages, Ruby felt about relationships.

'What do you think this outfit says about me!?' Madge would beg regardless.

'It says what all your outfits say about you, Mum.'

'Which is what?'

'That you're beautiful and wonderful and anyone would be lucky to have you.'

Ruby always needed to know exactly where Madge was going and what time she'd be back. She'd reiterate over and over again that they could still use their secret code if they needed to. If Madge ever found herself, again, at the unkind hands of an unkind man.

Madge started going out on the same nights of the week and taking calls at roughly the same time.

It became apparent that Madge was no longer meeting a rotation of new men, but the same guy.

It didn't come as a surprise when Madge put the idea out:

'I'd like us all to hang out, would you be up for that?'

'Oh God. Meet your boyfriend?'

'Well not, meet. You've met him hundreds of times.'

Ruby laughed for days when she realised her mum had been dating the fruit and veg man all along.

It made entire sense; the constant flow of plantain, and tomatoes.

And, more importantly, it put Ruby's anxious mind at ease.

She'd discovered the fruit and veg man in their very first week. He'd always been so helpful without ever being imposing. Magenta deserved that.

One evening Ruby had an idea about the box of gold gilt frames she'd kept under the bed since they moved. She was excited to tell her mum about it. But when Madge came home that night Ruby sensed change in the air, her stomach churned, she felt herself ready to run, already tying up her laces.

Without speaking Madge placed a small paper packet on the table.

'What's this?'
'It's a pattern for a wedding dress.'

Ruby was silent but in her mind she was already packing boxes.

Madge continued:

'I haven't said yes yet. . . I wanted to know what you think first. . .'
'Mum, you've got to do what makes you happy, we've both learned that right?'
'I knew you'd say that. I'm going to say yes.'

Ruby was trying to remember which removals van company was best.

'That's wonderful, Mum, really. . . so when do I need to move out?'

'What? Why would you do that. . .? Unless you want to leave. Do you?'

'No. No, I don't.'

Magenta swept Ruby up into arms and then said.

'Ok. Good. Because I've got huge plans for you.'

Madge suggested Ruby make the dress and a few days after that Madge said offhand,

'You know. . . I was thinking it might be nice if the whole thing was homemade? If we put it all together. . . if you put it all together?'

'Me?'

'Yes, you, Ruby. I was thinking, might be fun if everything was from the markets?'

The impracticalities of it all screamed at Ruby, but it was a gorgeous offer and she couldn't resist it.

When the gallery she was now working in said they'd happily lend her the space for the evening they were off and laughing. Ruby embarked on a buying and making expedition which took her from Tooting to Columbia Road, from East Street to Portobello. And even a few day trips out of town.

Just as exhaustion started to set in – three weeks before the wedding – Ruby and Madge had what they affectionately called a 'Mummy-moon'.

They did a series of things they felt they'd missed – things Ruby's father had forbidden.

They drove off to the seaside to eat alarming amounts of candy floss, crash into each other repeatedly on the bumper cars and whizz upside-down, inside-out on the biggest roller coasters.

And just as they could take no more sugar and deep-fried goods they checked into a spa.

They lay in lavender-scented relaxation pods sipping green juice, which meant they later found themselves in giddy hysterics as they uncontrollably farted into the bubbles of the jacuzzi.

And they didn't once feel any regret that they hadn't done any of these things sooner because in fact it was better. In that way that doing things to your own timeline, is always better.

The wedding was spectacular.

Sets of scales piled high with penny sweets and adorned in fake flowers formed the centrepieces of the four wallpaper tables at which their dearest friends and family sat.

Costume jewellery rings were exchanged.

A homemade cake was baked.

There was karaoke instead of a DJ.

At the end of the night, admiring how her fuchsia heels peeped out from the bottom of her orange dress, Ruby sat sipping her way towards a hangover she wouldn't regret.

Madge, giggling, strolled over and asked her daughter for one last dance of the night.

A cousin sang a song neither of them knew and an aunt set the bubble machine loose.
Ruby and Madge cackled, in that way that only Ruby and Magenta could, same shade but slightly different hue.

In the morning while the newlyweds slept and before they caught their honeymoon flight, Ruby laid out the project she'd been secretly working on since they'd moved in. The gold gilt frames. Each one now filled with a photo from one of their many beautiful days. She'd printed the photos and delicately embellished each image. Small painted details in each one. Embroidery in some. One was a collage of tickets to places they'd been to.

Humbled and astonished by the person she'd created, Madge cried her eyes out.
The fruit and veg man held them both in his arms.
Certainly funny how it worked out.

For someone who loved markets so much,
Ruby had never been one for stalling in a home too long
She had always thought survival meant leaving.

Sometimes, it's staying.

Hatty and the
Guy at Work

Hatty had met him at nineteen.

Her first job.

An office block.

Him, Al, twenty-six.

He was one of the pair who had interviewed her.

Two men.

Hatty staring back.

She'd done well, she knew she had.

But as soon as she'd walked out, realised she didn't have her headphones.

So turned back towards the interview room.

Couldn't resist eavesdropping through the door that had been left
a sliver ajar.

The most senior of the men said:

'She's young so at least we know she won't be getting pregnant and wanting mat leave. And pretty – always nice to have something pretty in the place.'

Al released a loud gruff sigh and admonished,

'Yup! Okay, that's another one of your classic inappropriate comments there. She's not an object.'

Hatty pushed the door open.
Wilfully expressionless but looking straight at Al.
Who was so unsure of whether she'd heard he pulled a few faces in a few seconds. Apologetic. Authoritative. Nothing to see here. Apologetic again.
She grabbed her headphones.
Walked back out.
Not letting on she'd heard at all.

Hatty walked away, wondering if his voice had always been so raspy.

Specifically, it was the way he rolled his 'R's that made her flutter. Starting every meeting 'Right, rrrrright. . .?' and opening his hands out to the team.
So, Hatty got to work, while also applying herself fully, to a task known well to many:

The art of getting to know a man.

The art of giving good questions so that you might get good answers. Only ever asking what you're willing to be asked back.

At the right intervals.

Without losing the element of surprise.

An art. A true art.

From the off, she loved to listen to him.

Especially when he led meetings and especially when he gave instructions.

There was an officiousness to him, a steeliness.

A sureness in him she'd not heard in anyone else.

Saying everything as though it was part of an agenda.

A plan.

And just the hint of a geography in his accent which took her somewhere new.

So after each meeting when they'd both head to the kitchen.

She would play dippy and ask him to explain, one more time, one more thing.

'Remind me again, when was that next big meeting? I personally liked the print assets but not so sure about the digital marketing? What are you thinking? What can we do to make sure the branding is really hitting?'

He would always answer her questions while already walking out the door.

And she liked the way he always left her wanting more.

One particular morning she found him pacing, exasperatedly, up and down the small square of the kitchen.

'Al, everything alright?' Hatty asked, reaching up for the sugar, taking out an earphone.

Avoiding the question he implored, 'What are you listening to?' In reply she flashed him her phone.

A look of surprise slid across his face as he took it brazenly from her and said,

> 'Interesting. That's one of my favourite albums – let's see what else you listen to, eh?'
> 'Cool.'

She tried to not look excited at all – tried to hide her sense of triumph.
Common ground. One of the pillars of the art.
She leaned against the counter, confidently and carefree as if to goad, 'Go on, judge me'.
At the best of times, she felt her music taste was unrivalled, but she currently, especially, knew if he liked that album, he'd love everything else there too.
Impressing him felt good. Really, really good.

From then on, he'd meet her there each morning and ask things like,

> 'Have you heard the new track from—? Oh, hang on I might as well just play it for you.'

And they'd shut the kitchen door and play the song on loud.
Those minutes made the commute, suit and re-heated lunch feel worth it.
The door to that kitchen became a gateway to a whole other world.
To conversations about what they liked.
And what they didn't.
Where they both grew up.
The ways their backstories were similar. The ways they weren't.

And every time she knew she'd impressed him a triumphant heat coursed through her body.

She took great joy in upping her game every day.

One morning she asked what he'd watched last night and when it transpired she'd already seen it, she remembered an interesting review so she'd said as offhand as she could:

'What's your number, I'll send you the link.'

And then time in the kitchen became a small part of their day, text messages soon took charge.

Every evening and on weekends too.

A constant flow of shared media sent with disclaimers like,

'Not to be devil's affogato because I know everyone hates it but personally, I think this is lowkey brilliant? What are your thoughts?'

And when the subject was something Al was passionate about – to Hatty's elation – he would record lengthy voice notes.

Hatty had always been the noisy one. The drama society one. The learning to play the drums one. The lets you know she's having – or not having – fun one. Now she contemplated if perhaps this had been a tactic to fill the silence. Perhaps she'd just never been interested in anyone like this? Because now Al had struck a chord with the listener in her, sitting back while he dominated the chat became one of her favourite pastimes. When she would flip the script and respectfully disagree, she got a kick from wondering if watching her win was one of his pastimes too.

For her twentieth birthday he sent her a playlist.
They weren't songs you'd listen to on your run.
Or on the commute.
They were songs you'd listen to in the deepest moments of the night.
They were rhythms to make a body unwind.
What she heard in every choice of track was,
I'm thinking about you. I'm thinking about you. I'm thinking about you.

Sometimes when Hatty was extra lucky, he would reply with videos, his face to camera.
Her phone forever on vibrate, his messages always coming in.
Recordings she'd play over and over again as she lay in bed.
She adored the idea that he might be doing the same with the videos she also sent.

An unspoken rule formed in the office that if Hatty and Al were in the kitchen everyone else would leave them to it.
Especially if it was one of the times they were in hot debate, disagreeing.
An Energy between them had been noted,
by Wendy from HR, especially,
there was something about the way they'd go for each other bar for bar
and then one night, for the first time since Hatty had joined the office, it was bar to bar
after work.
Spring.
So the air was blossoming with promise.
They'd just done well, a great deal signed.
So there were drinks.

And she looked good as she always did, and he looked better as he
always did.

And there were celebrations and smiles and '*oh we couldn't have done
this without you*'s.

And Al's hands grazed Hatty's knees.

And Hatty's gaze lingered more and more on his.

Words grew hot on hibiscus gin and tonic tongues.

When their colleagues started to disperse

Al and Hatty found the dancefloor.

Their bodies started to do what their conversations had been doing
in the kitchen.

Months of friction, sparking.

Limbs finishing sentences their lips had started.

Al in the lead.

And Wendy from HR – light-headed but always on the lookout –
said,

'Right. Let's call it a day!'

But the day was not called.

The company card was yet to be smacked down at least three more
times,

and falafel wraps were yet to be swallowed whole.

Someone was yet to scream-laugh as they dropped their chips

and there hadn't even been enough night yet for someone to say,

'It's so FUN to be out without the kids.'

And then it was 2 a.m..

And Hatty said,

'Shitttt, I left my house keys at the office.'

And Al said,

'That's cool I'll walk you back.'

In the morning they woke up under his desk as though some great war had broken out above them.
In a way it had.
In a way it was about to.
Before she had a chance to roll over and see his face, he said:

'Come on, we need to get up and get out so we can be back at nine like we haven't been here all night.'

On autopilot she straightened out her clothes and found herself halfway down the road, alone.

With no time to go home she sat in the window of the cafe on the corner. The paper bag of the croissant she'd just brought turning translucent in her hands.
Something, somewhere in her, told her she was soon to cry.

He started buying his coffee offsite instead, so no more excuses to use the kitchen each morning.

And that was how it went.

Occasionally there would be a reason to go to his office.
But he would always make a show of taking a call or responding to
an email he couldn't possibly look up from. It soon became apparent they were never going to talk about what happened so Hatty
did what she could to contain the fire she felt for him, shrinking it
to just an old flame.

One morning they were both walking along the same corridor,
hurt now, after her failed kiss chase, and just wanting to get away,
Hatty quickened her pace.
But her shoes were a tap too new, too slick on the sole,
She tripped.
Al watched her tumble the entire flight, in total horror,
never before had she looked so petite, so tiny, so five-foot-two,
he didn't get to her fast enough to catch her fall
saw her head slam into the floor
Embarrassed, still shocked, she tried to get up, but a dizziness spun
through her,
gravity collapsed her back down to the base of the steps.
Al's eyes watered as he panic-undid the top button of his collar.
Hatty dragged herself up, refusing to lean her weight against him,
rejecting his help.
For a second he watched her try to steady herself, but she was
wobbly, and nothing about her movements were making sense.

'This is silly,' he said.
'Let me!' he commanded.

With one motion he lifted her in her entirety, carried her to the front desk and called a cab that took them both to the hospital. She remembered all of his six-foot-three.

Sat in the waiting room, she allowed herself to lean on him as adrenaline began to fade. He called the office to explain their abrupt departure and when he hung up, she looked at him and feebly said, 'It's starting to hurt now'. He pulled her closer with a, 'Shhh shhh it will be okay, Hatty, don't worry,' and kissed her on the forehead. It wasn't a furtive kiss, or reluctant in the way he'd been the last few months. It was warm, close, the way he'd been with her that night under the desk.

He kept his lips pressed there a long time, both their hearts racing.

She closed her eyes, sunk closer into him and sighed,

'Talk to me about what to do after a concussion, Al, is that ten hours thing true – do I need to stay awake for ten hours now, just in case?'

As it turned out, it wasn't true, not exactly. He did need to make sure she didn't sleep for too long at a time though. They went back to the flat she lived in alone, watched films and listened to albums in her room. As night started to fall, he got up to go, said he'd call every hour. Hatty said,

'Al, I need you to stay.'

So he slid into her bed. Grey suit still on. Al set alarms that woke them up once every few hours. During these intervals they talked about things neither of them would remember.

In the morning she woke up to find him scoring the underside of her shoes with his keys.

'Al? What on earth are you doing?'
'I'm putting the grip back in. I don't want to see you hurt yourself again.'

Still slumped, she crashed back into her pillows to sleep. He went back to work, messaging her throughout the day to check she was okay.

By the end of the week, when he was sure she was, he went back to ignoring her completely.

*

At the end of summer, for the company's 30th anniversary they all went on a corporate glamping retreat.
For weeks, Hatty's inbox had been clogged with:

Tina, 10:53 a.m.:	What if it rains!?! Should we bring wellies. . .
Steve, 10:56 a.m.:	Best to be prepared, I'm bringing my orthopaedic pillow too, it cost £90
Tina, 10.59 a.m.:	NINETY QUID? Gosh.
Tina, 11:00 a.m.:	Sorry forgot to ask. . . Who is bringing the sun cream?
Lauren, 11:30 a.m.:	No! Everyone bring their own sun cream! WE ARE ALL RESPONSIBLE FOR OURSELVES.
Steve, 11:40 a.m.:	What if it's cold?

Wendy, 11:45 a.m.:   OMG HEATWAVE FORECAST GUYS.

Hatty didn't care because she had put herself forward to make the playlists. And she wanted to get this perfect. She'd sent an email survey around the office, asked everyone to send over three songs they'd love to hear and with that she made three perfect playlists with very different moods: journey there, BBQ party, journey back.

She sat at the back of the coach on the way out of the city, and allowed herself to be showered in praise as colleague after colleague piped up 'Yesss Hatty, this is MY tune!' She hadn't needed to ask Al to tell her what he'd choose, because she already knew, but the brief email exchange about his three songs gave her butterflies, still.

For her retreat activities Hatty chose 'mindful walking'. Which is what she needed: a break from the blaze of thoughts in her head and some fresh air. For the afternoon she picked 'flower crown making' because she knew, categorically, that Al wouldn't be there.

By the second day, the impact of not being in the city felt amazing, the pollution-free skies and bird song had worked magic. She felt glad she'd kicked up a fuss, dug her heels in and refused to share her bell tent with anyone else.
Smugly, on the airbed she slipped into the outfit for the BBQ she'd spent weeks agonising over. Smart-casual being her least favourite dress code. Casual-casual she could do. And smart-smart she was excellent at. But smart-casual always eluded her slightly.
A wide-legged white jumpsuit with gold trainers and a hopeful smile.

She wondered if Al would notice her tonight. And then told herself off for thinking about him at all.

At the food tables a succulent bite of gossip was being chewed over: Tina was enjoying telling everyone that Steve, who always makes out he's so outdoorsy and such a big LAD'S lad, had apparently, 'LITERALLY shit himself during the abseiling session.' Lauren confirmed and Hatty laughed, really laughed.

As the fire pits were lit, partners and families arrived to join the final night. Bunting and fairy lights hung loosely through the trees and the sky was an ombré of orange and pink. As Hatty daydreamed into the oncoming night, snapping photos of the marshmallow circle of tents in the distance, a group nearby were getting loud about something that was polarising, clearly.

She heard her name fly through the balmy night.

'Hatty! Al is talking absolute rubbish. Put him in his place, please!?'

Next to Al was a woman Hatty hadn't seen before.
Before anyone had a chance to say anything the woman said,

'Ohhhhh, hi, Hatty, is it? I'm the fiancée! Hi!'

Sliding her arm into Al's as she spoke. Al stood there, stiff as the plastic groom on a cake stopper.

Hatty noted the stealthy job the fiancée had done of coming across cute while marking her territory.

All Hatty could hear was the penny dropping.

Not so much a penny, but the clatter of many: that arcade game, where you slot in coin after coin until they all come crashing down and you win a keyring, sprang to mind. And the pennies just kept on dropping and dropping. *Exactly!* she thought. It was exactly like that game: you keep getting out what you put in. Pennies out, pennies in. You just keep playing these games over and over again. These stupid games with stupid men. She'd never asked if he was in a relationship. And he had never said.

Later, Wendy from HR found Hatty perched on a tree stump. She scooched onto it next to her.
'You okay?' she asked. Hatty nodded. Wendy from HR said, 'I'm sorry. . . we thought you knew. . .'

By winter, Hatty had a new job.

Al wrote her a reference that was so kind, observant and appreciative that she couldn't tell if it was because he felt these things or if he just really wanted her out of the office.

Months passed quickly and they both settled into a pattern without each other's presence always posing a question mark. The circles of their mutual work friends overlapped enough for her to know his wedding never happened and they were both still in the same city.

As the years went on Hatty got just enough intel on Al, so presumably Al got what he needed about Hatty.

And then further into her twenties, having amassed a few more heartaches, Hatty bumped into Al on the train. They talked briefly about what they'd both been up to (both pretending that the information was new) and then Al realised he hadn't turned his music off.
'Oh, what are you listening to?' asked Hatty.
And in that way that things sometimes do, they started up again.

This time Hatty approached Al not so much as a red flag, but as a set of traffic lights. She chose to afford him grace at this crossroads, hoping he'd shine amber in the golden sunset glow and eventually go green. They never talked about what had happened the first time round or the spaces in between.

One Thursday, deep into their summer they laughed more than they usually did.
Drove – music blaring in the car – until they reached a seaside town.
Proper fish and proper chips.
He smiled at her more than he usually did.
They shared so many laughs that day it was as though a single stress had never passed between them.
Hatty remembers feeling easy, free.
It was to be one of the most stunning days of her life.
He placed his hand in hers and he looked at her for a long time.
Deeper and deeper in the blue of her eyes.

She said she'd text him when she's home and see him in the week.
But as she walked away, a feeling found her, one she'd known once
before.
She held back a tear,
the origin of which she couldn't quite find.
But something, somewhere in her, told her she was soon to cry.

He fizzled her out in flurry of,

'I'm not ready.'
'There are loads of other things I want to do before settling
down.'
'I want to go travelling. . . we can't be together if I'm travelling.'

And now it's nine years since she walked into that office.

And they're very much in touch but very much apart.

Hatty is explaining it – reluctantly – to a new colleague.

'Right. So, what's happening now?'
'Nothing much, he's away.'
'So he did at least go travelling?'
'No he didn't. Just away for a couple weeks.'

And the colleague wants to be a friend.
Wants to be useful.
But she also knows this life is complex.
That we can never really know what happens between two people,
and good advice is so much more than what she reads 45 times a

day in neat Instagram infographics. She sees in Hatty one of the most powerful women she knows.

And she can tell that dinner by dinner, dessert by dessert the two of them will get closer and closer.

She can see exactly why Al won't let Hatty go but she wishes he would.

Before she can formulate a response or even a question, Hatty says,

> 'I think of us as an orchid. Once beautiful, now dormant. Or maybe we are more like an amaryllis? I know they're basically the same. . . Aren't they? I dunno. An orchid does its own thing, I think. Whereas an amaryllis has to be cared for a bit. There's a bit more process to it. My plant mummying is poor. . . but yeah. . .'

Hatty knows they're going to be good friends because the colleague strives to understand.

She watches as the colleague tries to come back with something. Hatty feels obliged to admit,

> 'I know it's not normal. But to be honest normal has not been that kind to me either.'

And the colleague says,

> 'Oh, trust me, I get that.'

And the cupcake listens. And the matcha latte applauds.

I. Get. That.

Three of the most important words one woman can say to another.

Hatty sighs in relief.

'In other news: this cafe is shit.'

The colleague laughs because it really really is.

They both glare admonishingly at the special they ordered which looks like folded laundry and tastes like it too.

On the walk home Hatty ponders what her life with Al could actually look like. Has she ever asked what he thinks of marriage? She's definitely never asked if he wants kids. She wonders how it would feel to not to be tethered to someone like this. It's like being tethered to a balloon. Initially appearing featherlight and free. But really just fragile to the breeze.

Hatty climbs to the top deck of the bus and checks her phone.

She flicks through the apps. Someone shouts about how much frozen yogurt tastes like white chocolate. Someone else shares a gorgeous selfie after a flight, which bewilders her because she enters planes like a fresh grape and by the time she exits she's as dehydrated as a raisin.

She tries to resist the urge to do so, but closes her eyes and listens to Al's last voicenote.

And then her phone vibrates.

It's Al.

'Haha, your ears must have been burning.'

'Oh, talking about me, were you? All good things I hope?'

'Oh, always.'

'Good, good. Anyway, I'm home next week, fancy a drink?'

But for the first time since she's known him, Hatty doesn't feel so certain of immediately saying yes.

Dia is a Leader

A big woman, literally, tall, commands a lot of space

But she wears a lot of layers

So people always wonder what's underneath

Despite themselves, always curious about what she looks like naked, as though she's property

Looking at her the way they would were she the vases or the statues in a museum.

It's caused her problems in more ways than one,

Especially for her son, whose friends enjoy winding him up: asking questions like, 'How does it feel to be the son of a MILF?'

Dia is trying to teach Cub not to bat an eyelid. And, ever her student, he's trying to learn.

His mother has always been his hero, the bravest, realest, coolest person he knows.

She has so many stories and he appreciates them all. He just wishes she would tell them all.

'Which is where my podcast would come in,' he keeps hinting.

Cub has a podcast.

'The Cubcast' – he regrets the name slightly now, feels it's too self-centred now but they're ten episodes in, and it's doing pretty well. A steadily growing audience.

He set it up with Blue. A father–son chat-show type thing.

Cub was disheartened with everything he was hearing about all the problems of the world around him

And just as this threatened to make him disconnect and despair, Blue suggested, 'Maybe more people think like you than you realise, maybe they just need to hear from you.'

In the early stages Dia didn't understand exactly what a podcast was. Cub had explained, or tried to,

'It's like the radio, but without scheduling. It's like the radio, but at your fingertips. . . on your phone.'

She was none the wiser, but she knew if he was anything like her (and he was) that he needed space to explore, to work himself out. As a child she had always been told little girls shouldn't be too loud, as a teenager she'd always been hushed. So if he wanted to talk, then let him talk.

She watched as her boys took the empty shed at the end of the garden and turned it into a den-slash-studio for them both.

Unfortunately, they did so in one of those excruciatingly hot UK summer weeks. When everyone says, 'We wanted the sun, but not like this'. Dia kept fretting they'd overheat so constantly produced new ice lolly experiments for them in between running her own sessions in the house.

When their first episode came out, Dia listened to it in the kitchen as she unloaded the dishwasher.

She stopped several times, to nod, to rewind, to digest.

Her son's openness and their candid chats about the issue of the day blew her away.

She purchased them a mini fridge because this was going to be more than a phase and she couldn't keep running up and down the garden every Saturday.

She wanted to leave them to it, let them have their thing. But they had other ideas.

'Mum. Please! Can I interview you?'

'Me? About what?'

'About everything you do, this place, our home, the workshops and all the reasons: your life.'

'My life?'

'Yeah. Your life. I think the listeners, all of us, would get a lot from it. Think about it, okay?'

He says it as though him and Blue haven't already drafted the questions out.

That night, Dia talks it over with Blue.

'Do you think it's a good idea?'

'I do. Don't you?'

It worries her to be so public about the things she's been through. but it worries her more to let her son down.

'Heavy is the head that wears a crown,' she sighs.

'When raising such a smart, curious, young king,' Blue replies.

Over breakfast she announces, 'Okay, today's the day.'

Cub's eyes light up and she looks at him now.

Gangly, very gangly.

Tall, like her, of course he would be.

His skin a shade entirely his own, unlike either of theirs.

He is his mother's son, she often jokes,

before concluding, he is the culmination of them both.

*

Cub introduces, 'Hello listeners, she's finally here – the woman you've all been asking for. Welcome to the Studio – formerly known as the shed. Let's talk about "HOME". Tell us how it came about, how you set it up?' Asks Cub, initiating the interview with his favourite story.

> 'Ha okay straight in! Hello! So. . . I was doing pretty well as a
> personal trainer, but I wanted to leave London. I was feeling
> isolated there. And I had always wanted to create space for
> people.'

On one of their first dates, Blue asked Dia what she dreamed for her life.

She wanted to help people heal, survive, learn.

In a space of her own. Alternative to the ones she'd already experienced.

Blue had been the first person she'd told her dream to who hadn't shrugged it off. Instead, he'd said,

> 'A home from home? You could definitely convert a house –
> look at what dentists do all the time.'

'Exactly' she laughed, aware she was falling in love, and also aware that because of that she was sharing a lot. She noted the way Blue held each clue about her. She valued the way he didn't push.

When their relationship became serious, he made it a daily habit to check the property pages.

Until one day they were being toured around a large

Georgian house,
even though it was in a town where the most exciting credential
was a pasty shop.
They could make it work, they knew.
Within weeks the paperwork was signed
and soon after that they were settling in
Pushing Cub on a new set of swings,
making friends with a new set of parents.
The pasty shop, soon after, lost its lease, but in the end it didn't
matter because the most exciting thing in the town would turn out
to be these three.
HOME, Dia's centre, became the place everyone talked about,
and over sixteen years, the beating heart of the entire town.
Cub asks: 'So, tell us a bit more about what you do?'

 'Self-love, self-acceptance, stuff around wellness, safety. One
 of the most popular workshops is my body-acceptance class
 where I invite the participants to compliment each other until
 they all stop blushing and start actively agreeing.'
 'How did these workshops come about? What inspired you?'
 'Well, with the body acceptance stuff, you know what it's like,'
 she replies.

Which of course her child does.
Noticing more and more the way his peers are becoming less free.
The small community he's grown up in so different to the world
of Dia and Blue
who grew up on two opposite ends of the tube map, always found
each other in the middle.
Cub navigates a totally different circle.
On days when the heat boils,
his friends wear more and more.

They go to the beach and refuse to take their t-shirts off,
seawater-soaked fabric oppressively clinging to their skin,
hiding their chests because they're embarrassed that they aren't
like the men in the films.

'Exactly!'

'I've always felt other people's eyes on me.'

Cub leans in. 'And how does that make you feel? That constant gaze?'

'I'm used to it. It's all I've known'

The image of herself once a month sat on the bench watching her
blissfully pre-pubescent classmates enjoy swimming lessons while
she had to suffer what felt like the consequences of growing, one of
the images of herself that remains most unerring.

'I've always been treated as freakish by some, desirable
by others.'

'Which do you think is worse?' interjects Blue.

'I don't know. I don't actually know.' Dia confesses.

Cub underlines something in his notebook, and Dia doesn't notice,
which is an excellent sign. Because things don't tend to pass her
by. He folds his arms and asks, 'and where do you think all that
comes from?'

She snorts on a sip of coffee.

'Where *doesn't* it come from!?'

When she was growing up bodies like hers, in magazines and the
press,

were treated as grotesque.

People blame social media now

but the problem has always been there.

Cub asks, 'Would you say there's been progress?'

'Still a way to go, but yeah. The woman who sold younger
me breakfast in a bottle so I wouldn't end up like one of those
poor sad celebrities who 'let themselves go'? I don't think they're
as exciting now. Their red circles of shame in the cheap mags
are condemned now'

Cub asks: 'Do you still feel eyes on you?'

'I do, but also, I don't care. My body is about more than what
it looks like. Has been through more than meets the eye'

Stretch marks streak Dia's body like the markings of a tiger.

A fierceness to match.

When the summer sun passes through their bedroom window her
scars shine rose gold across her skin

like the cracks of a vase which has been broken and fixed, broken
and fixed, broken and fixed.

Cub isn't ready yet to go where he knows Dia is taking the conversation so he says;

'Let's talk about love.

About relationships.'

Dia had started off odd at 18, a relationship with a boy she loved
but had to love in secret,

on account of her strict parents.

Parents who impressed upon her over and over that the life she
wanted wasn't right,

so Dia did what Dia had to do.

Dia learned to lie.

Dia still doesn't like talking about this now.

Because the lying didn't come easy to a soul as sure and pure as hers.

She regrets, still, that her earliest relationships should have felt joyful

But, instead, were ultimately just stressful.

'I couldn't wait to move out.'

'I can imagine,' says Cub, knowing full well he actually can't imagine it at all.

'The thing about those households is that even after you get out, the judgement they instilled in you hangs around.'

And that took a lot from Dia,
It took the glow of the mornings after.
It took her ability to ask for help.
It meant she always held herself to blame.
It meant the feeling she knew most had always been shame.
It took energy to live a full life regardless of that pain,
But she persisted, energetic, day after day.
Searching for satisfaction or love or something in between, date after date.
And yes, initially, it was fun
to always be the one
with the stories.
The one
through whom your married friends lived vicariously.

'But the truth was when I turned thirty, being that one felt lonely. The shadows of my past were growing more present by the day. When I blew the candles out on my cake I looked around the room. And felt totally exhausted. I barely had the strength to wish (but of course I did).'

Dia belonged to the generation just before everyone went to therapy.
And her mother belonged to the generation that said,
'Well What Did You Expect Going Out Like That'.
So it took grit to go to the dismissive doctor's office and say words

which were still taboo.

'I need to talk to someone about some things that have happened to me'

Cub doesn't want to ask it, but knows he has to.

'Could you talk a bit about what those things were?'

Dia's truth starts to uncoil now. It lays itself flat in the space across them all. Cub contemplates changing the subject, not because he doesn't want to hear it, but because his instinct always flares towards protecting his mum. He wishes he could somehow go back in time and stop the things that happened to her from happening.

Blue reads him knowingly, remembering how he had felt when Dia first told him.

Blue looks at him in a way that says, *I know you can do this.*

Dia takes Blue's hand, locks her fingers into his and speaks.

Dia's favourite word is 'consent',

she leads a workshop on it.

    'Consent,' she repeats.

    'Consent,' she says again.

Drumming into the boys how to check and double check.

Drumming into the girls that they should only act on the most enthusiastic of yes.

But also in Dia's mind – not at the front – not at the back either – but somewhere always to the side –

is an echo

of herself,

aged twenty-five:

'No.'

'No, I said no.'

Over and over again, until her throat hurt.

'No, please, stop, please.'

And then the hottest shower she can remember and the way she'll never again use the fabric softener that smells like freshly cut grass.

'And that's why I teach a self-defence class

I run a section on making sure you don't get grabbed by your scarf, and if they go for the back of your hair, don't run forward, throw yourself back into their body fast.

Know how to left-hook;

Use your knees;

Hold your keys, just in case you need to fight;

Have someone's number on speed dial, in fact, have mine;

Know that there's a big difference between the fastest route home and the safest;

Take the path where the lights are brightest;

And get acquainted with the owner of the shop which closes last;

And don't forget, don't forget, don't forget,

Just because you said yes in the taxi doesn't mean you can't change your mind in the bed.

Just because he says he loves you doesn't mean you owe him sex.

Just because he's your partner doesn't mean he can.

Just because he's a friend doesn't mean he won't.

Just because it's easiest to blame yourself, doesn't mean you should.

Just because the first person didn't listen, doesn't mean you won't eventually be understood.

Just because you feel lonely doesn't mean you are alone.

I want all your futures to be different to my past.

I want you to shine, but not because you've known the dark.

So here I am ready with a hug, but also, showing you how to

break a rib with one shove.'

Though none of this is new information to her son, Cub still sniffles just enough that the mic picks it up. Dia brushes a knuckle under his chin. The three of them sit in a chain of tenderly grazed hands for a second before Dia forges on.

'So yeah, I had to make myself better, we say 'healing' now, but that language didn't exist for me. And it was a real surprise when, at thirty three, I started a dalliance with Blue.'

Cub invites. 'Go on, tell us more?'

'It really *was* a surprise: we met at the gym.'

Cub directs the next question to his dad.

'What was your opening line again?'

'Don't forget to protect your thumb.'

After watching her punch and punch and punch the bag
Cub, laughing, asks,
'And that was what did it for you?'
'Well, yeah. It was the surprise of not feeling patronised. I still found myself apologising and your dad said if we're going to be friends, promise to never apologise for your fury.'
For Blue, Dia felt a striking certainty.
She didn't know if the relationship would last forever, but she knew, just knew,
that the love would.
It was him, she knew, after just a few months,
    with the way he communicated clearly, loved carefully and
    cared greatly,
    with the way he believed what she believed just as deeply,
    with the way he knew how to challenge her intelligently

and fairly

and could always tell when she needed to be cradled wholly, kissed squarely, laid down gently.

He always read the many rooms of her, deftly.

And never once had she needed to show him how.

And so everything with Blue felt spacious, felt free, felt expansive.

'And it meant a lot to me to not feel limited.'

Having known so much of the opposite – here Blue was, one of the good ones.

Her the tiger, him the unicorn.

It wasn't easy, obviously.

It took months and months to come together.

He had things to do

and so did she.

Other cities he worked in.

With anyone else she might have thought him to be lying,

but something in her knew he was the real thing,

when he said he was busy, he meant it,

and whatever he said to her, it wasn't that she heard it, it was that she felt it.

So yes, it was him, she knew, after just a few months.

And it was to him she told the thing she held back from almost everyone:

what I want, what I really want, is to be a mum

And he nodded and said, 'I see that for you, I see that for us,'

they agreed.

Let's always be like this,

let's always do this our way

'You took ages – Cub – but we really enjoyed making an
immediate start.'
Cub cringes into the mic.

'Sorry, sorry. I couldn't resist. Anyway, it took four years
to actually happen.'
It also took a loss
The kind of which is hard to fully express,
especially for someone like Dia who had always been more body
than words

It would creep up on her when watching a film or a soap
She'd stiffen up at the screen, close her eyes, predict the plot

'Their baby is going to die' she'd whisper,
and Blue would place his hand on top of hers,
The lifeline of his palm pressing against her clenched fist
He'd run the pads of his fingertips across her knuckles
Gently feel through the spaces in between
She would count *one, two, three. One, two, three*
Until she could bring herself to loosen her grip
Just enough for him to slide his fingers in between hers.
She would close her fingers around his,
and they would hold each other's hands tightly,
Sharing each other's energy until they felt some stability,
Until they felt steady
Until Dia was ready to turn her palm so it touched his,
And Blue would eventually raise her hands to his lips and seal their
pain with a kiss.

Cub says with real maturity now,

'It must have taken courage to try again and again?'

'It did – and I was also just so angry.'

She couldn't believe how little she'd been taught about the effort to get pregnant. Or how to cope with the loss. And then being expected to move on and just try again.

She was angrier than she'd ever been and that was really something.

'I couldn't stop asking, why had no one fucking talked about this?'

And for the first time she found herself fearing, genuinely, fearing

She was at the fifth birthday party of a friend's daughter when she heard a whisper from the other mothers.

'Dia still can't get pregnant'

'Well, at the end of the day, she really did leave it late.'

The nattering summoned the memory of chlorine,

She felt herself sat to the side,

watching the others swimming.

Wondering why, her body wasn't behaving

again.

It took a lot from Dia:

those lines on the stick never quite appearing

And the doctor's resigned words, 'Nothing seems to actually be wrong, it's just not sticking.'

'So what happened?' (He tries to ask this as though he doesn't know the answer)

'We *were* advised to accept the ache of our life not clicking. But. . .'

One night they were at the gym,

She sat balanced on the exercise ball, and Blue was rowing.

She watched the motion of his body,

Her favourite part of him: his back.

The precision of his shoulder blades,

the tattoos she knew by heart,

his slick sweat as familiar as her own,

that back she'd watched paint walls and grout tiles.

She sat watching it now, hoping and hoping that back would one day lift a child.

She contemplated how tired that back must be from carrying her, himself, it all.

'What are you thinking, Dia?' he panted between sips from a metallic bottle.

In an automatic motion he offered his water to her and she took it, eyes fixed on him as she drank.

The worry lines the years had gifted him.

The comfortable gleam of a head retired from the efforts of growing hair.

His powerful beard, it's wiry grey strands.

Blue, her silver lining.

She watched his gaze go from gentle to uncompromising.

'Come on Dia, tell me what you're thinking. . . get it off your chest'

'You can leave, you know?' She finally said.

   'I know I can. But why would I do that?'

'Because you want a baby, and I'm not. . . It's not. . .'

'I want a baby with you, Dia, and only you.'

A smile broke across her face the way the sun breaks through the clouds.

Dia knew then: that either way they would both be fine.

And the only thing Blue adored more than seeing Dia smile was the knowledge that it was him that made her smile. And then she sighed.

A sigh Blue knew.

A sigh that's a yearn.

She leaned forward, and whispered gently into his neck,

that sigh soaking deep into his flesh.

'Meet me in the family cubicle, Blue.'

Now, Blue jumps at the opportunity to make a dad joke.

'Considering the conception, we should have called you Jim!'

'Ugh. Dad. Anyway. What happened next?'

'Well, then. When you were about two, a few insidious look-ing cells meant I needed a hysterectomy. And I ended up getting blasted into menopause early. My body pressed fast forward again, and I was experiencing something totally different to everyone else. Again!'

Dia pauses.

'But that's just the way life goes?

Everyone's story is different. Some of us have lived more stories than others.

I've lived a lot of life.

Most women have.

And so much of it could have been easier.

We have so many questions, but are we always met with answers?

We go it alone too often.

So I want to make things easier for others.

We shouldn't just strive to feel safe.

Safe is the minimum.

The goal is to feel empowered.
Powerful.
So that's why I do what I do.
As I said there're classes for the men too, because men are
part of this. Men need to be better.
So I'm keeping that class on consent.
And I'm going to teach the self defence
even if I hate having to teach it
because someone has to and that someone is me'
'Wow, what a note to end on thanks Mum, Dia.'
When Cub stops recording, Dia gets up and leaves. Cub looks
concerned, worried he asked too much, but Blue reassures him, he
knows Dia's wild well, she just needs to take herself off to the woods,
as it were, for some alone time. To breathe, to just be. Blue knows
that later that night she'll hold onto him tightly until she falls asleep.

*

When it's time to listen to the conversation back, Dia is reminded
they filmed it too, and this adds something new, something she
wasn't sure she wanted to see.
To start with she watches it as though the words came from someone else's mouth.
And then she starts to hear herself.
Impressed that she managed to articulate everything she meant.
She hears each story of all the women she's been, in the last five
decades.
She always imagines herself as looking scatty, a bit of a wreck, but
looking now she only sees her resilience shining back. She sees the
person she always wanted to be.

Blue enters the studio and watches over her shoulder as she sees herself through her family's eyes for perhaps the first time. He kisses her on the back of the head and says:

'You're amazing.'

And she agrees.

She wishes there had been someone like her around when she was a young woman.

She has so much to say now that her rage has changed shape.

Now that it's no longer brittle,

now that she's soft.

A something flexible, with motion, that she can channel

and has channelled

and will channel.

Cub joins them and asks her what she thinks, and she tells him he's done a wonderful job.

Dia and Blue hold each other's gaze,

they comprehend the boy they made,

The man he's growing into.

The dream of him, something they are so glad they held on to.

Their hands follow each other's across the table, like the ticking arms of a clock.

Cub had the instinct the episode would do well, but not as well as this.

Now Dia finally sees herself, so does everyone else.

Every day her audience increases.

And though she's of the exact age that doesn't quite understand what an influencer does,

she does reply to all her direct messages,

because this, she can get to grips with.

Because she knows exactly what it means when woman after woman messages her saying,

> *Thank you so much for saying this.*
> *It resonates more than I can say.*

A 'Dear Dia' blog is suggested by a well-known magazine. She's even approached about a book deal, which she says no to because writing isn't her thing and she is forever being invited to speak on other people's podcasts.

The questions tend to vary but one thing they do always wonder is:

> *What is the most important lesson you've learnt?*

And she always says the same exact thing.

> 'You can't be in charge of the time,
> but you do have to trust the timing.'

Ash and Han

Ash has been waiting for Han for an hour.

Usually this is fine because Ash will bring snacks and a bit of work to do, some reading or a list of emails to flick through. But Han had promised to be on time. Though Ash has a lot on her plate, it was effort enough – in streams of half-read messages – to even save the date, let alone re-arrange.

And crucially, she thought Han would show up on time – or at least she'd hoped.

Ash met Han at university.

Not in the usual way. Not in the way of glow sticks and shot glasses.

No, it was a life drawing class,

eyes meeting across a voluminous naked arse.

One sketching in charcoal, the other in oil pastel.

One quite good,
The other brilliant.
Han taking the piss
while Ash focused.
Han fluttered her way in with a blagged free pass,
whereas Ash had saved, signed up and committed to each and
every class.

One week they all turned up to find their teacher had cancelled.
Han suggested they all go to the pub instead,
and Ash jumped at the chance because, so far, she hadn't done the
best job of making friends.
By the third round of cider and black Ash and Han were fascinated
by each other.
Making each other laugh in the corner,
discovering a shared sense of humour,
they left last, swapped numbers and started meeting up on campus.
Always being hushed in the library and racing to the student bar
after lectures.

They were best together when they were hungover.
Both liked their personal space but neither liked being totally alone
either,
so they'd sit on the same blue sofa
but at separate ends,
a wall of snacks between them.
    Pyjamas and pasta,
      last night's make up rubbed into the pillow,
      last night's outfit strewn across the floor.

They would watch sitcoms or makeover shows and they would never
ever, ever, debrief about the night before.
Ash knew that, for Han, the night out was always a blur as soon as
it was done,

> she was one of those people who would sit an exam and
> then all thought of it would leave her head.

Ash, on the other hand, would agonise throughout and then re-
agonise again about what she remembered writing for question x,
y and z.

> What Ash lost sleep over, Han had already forgotten
> What Ash thought about most, Han was barely
> bothered by.

One lived a life without accountability.
The other was detail, replay and memory.

> Except for when she couldn't bear to be

Exams tended to tear the tender in them apart:
Because Ash was a clever girl for sure, but also, she worked hard,
really hard.
Han would sit in the sun all day reading non-coursework books,
while Ash was always deep in her studies, deeper in her thoughts,
not just because she wanted the grades, but because she needed a
way out.

For Han, university was just something to do, because why not?
But Ash was the first in her family to be there, so it really meant
something, it meant a lot.

Ash wanted to make her mark, wanted to be part of creating a better world.
On her back were things she ached to start and cycles she yearned to stop.

In her heart there were things she was scared to want.

Some days all of this added up to too much.
Too much responsibility,
too much tide to change,
too much too close, yet, too much out of range,
and it was on those days that Han would be most amazing,
would sweep in with prosecco and crisps, reminding Ash she didn't owe anyone anything.
It was on those days, Han showed Ash how to be selfish
and Ash had been grateful for this.

Through these moments Ash had come to learn:
prioritising her needs was a particular way to break a particular curse,
but she didn't notice how innately and inherently Han always put herself first.

In truth, neither had ever had a friend like the other
And the joy of that contrast had lasted many years.

Once upon a time Ash had decided that Han was helping her become her own person.
With Han she didn't need to be the eldest daughter.

No responsibilities to fulfil and no example to set.

When she was with Han, all Ash had to do was enjoy one haphazard night out after the next.

Han always encouraging Ash to tell her family she wouldn't be home again this weekend with a quick text:

'That way they won't plead with you down the line, and you can decide when to reply.'

Ash would feel uncertain, but Han would roll cigarettes and say,

'It's fine, it's fine,

you're changing the narrative.'

They'd had very few conversations about each other's home lives.

And yet, Han was always certain she knew all of Ash's story.

So what was it that made Han feel so qualified?

Thinking about it now, Ash knows the answer is stereotypes.

She hates that she let her family down all those times.

The thought makes all the muscles in Ash's jaw go hard.

Her shoulders try to meet her ears.

She becomes inordinately aware of her chest.

Of her heart beating inside said chest.

She realises she's been ripping the menu.

She looks at the tatters on the table and feels embarrassed.

She thinks about her lungs, she wonders if they peer through the French door slats of her rib cage and wonder what the fuck is going on out there? She imagines them as a pair of nosy neighbours complaining about all the pollution and smoking outside.

She thinks about the way the heart is a muscle.

She doesn't want hers to keep aching like this.

Being constantly let down by the person who is meant to be her best friend has made Ash feel weaker and weaker – so she is considering now what she needs to do to make herself stronger –

'Hiya – just checking if I can get you anything?'

A new waitress, different to the one who showed her to the table, arrives. Her hair is a gala of purples and her smile subtle.
She pours Ash a fresh glass of water. In the middle of the carafe is a large and phallic piece of coal. The waitress is trying not to look at it, but Ash is fixated. Their eyes meet in the middle and they share a laugh. The waitress explains,

'It purifies the water. Apparently.'

They share another laugh as the waitress begins to tell Ash that there's been a change.

'There certainly has,' Ash says, accidentally out loud.
'. . . In that brunch has turned to lunch. . . But you look like brunch wasn't doing it for you anyway.'

The waitress picks up the shreds of paper and asks

'Do you have any dietary requirements?'

'It's nice to be asked,' thinks Ash as she has a flashback of a party at Han's parents' house
(which was neat and all fresh flowers-y. Filled with photos of every-

where Han and her family had been, whereas Ash's was full of pictures of the places they're from).

Ash was at the buffet
when Han's aunt introduced herself.

'Lovely to meet you, I'm Ash.'
'Oh. That's a lovely nickname, but what were you Christened?'
'Errr. . . no, I wasn't Christened anything.'

Ash left some space for the lady to think again but she just looked blank, and then:

'Anyway, would you like a slice of the ham?'
'Ha, you're really not getting it, are you?'

The aunt had gawped on, confused.
Then Han came over giggling at the reprimand she could see brewing in Ash's eyes and whispered:

'Oh, come on Ash, not everyone knows someone like you!'

Mid mouthful of brie:
'Someone like me?'

Han could have said something – anything – useful. But she didn't.
She just laughed
Rolled her eyes in her aunt's direction and led Ash away.

With retrospect, sometimes it felt like Han wore Ash like a badge.

With retrospect, no one ever asked Han, what Han was short for.

Ash lingers on that thought before looking back up and remember-ing the waitress is there, something, clearly, on the tip of her tongue.

'You know what I've always thought?'
'Go on?'
'We should have a special. . . for dates. . . who've been stood up.'
'You should! But what would that be?'
'Maybe. . . a platter for one? Why should people sharing get all the fun?'
'That's actually great. But to be fair, I'm not waiting for a date.'
'You're not?'
'Nah, course not: would have left aaaages ago if I was.'
'Then what?'
'I'm waiting for a friend.'
'Shit! I'm so sorry. That's much worse.'

Ash lets out a weird involuntary noise, something that's tricky to describe but just comes out of her, something quietly animal, both certain and dismal. The waitress doesn't know how to respond, her inability to hold back is something she's been warned about before. But the words are out there now, nothing left to claw back. And they're both stuck there in this moment now which is absolutely absolute. In this moment where something has been said which is undeniably true.

Ash picks up the drinks menu.
Orders a cocktail and sighs.

'You're right, it actually is worse.'

At the start of each new year Ash and Han would debrief on how
their Christmases had gone: really different affairs.
One lunch served at midday,
the other a dinner at 7 p.m..
One with canapes,
the other with rice.
One where the family, took the whole week off – of course,
the other with dad doing a night shift, because a day 'doing English'
is more than enough.
But both were filled with love,
and together they loved that contrast.
Christmas was the sweet spot on the axis (if their friendship was
a graph)

Each year Ash would buy herself a diary,
a ritual she adored dearly.
Calendars and schedules and times were important to her,
she wanted to be booked, she wanted to be busy.
She'd always choose something she'd hope would reflect the year
ahead.
Affirming to herself: this year will be glittery or floral or bound in
leather.

One time Ash went to the loo and while she was gone Han grabbed
her diary and initiated a new tradition.

She'd embellish a whole week in biro bubble letters and year-six stars:

HAN'S BIRTHDAY WEEK

She'd add other things in too, on random weekends.

Don't forget to call Han today she needs you.

It was mostly cute, it was mostly cute, it was mostly cute.

But

Once, Ash was in a meeting for her first real job and they'd asked her to clarify some dates, pulling out the diary she was met with:

LET'S GET SO DRUNK THIS WEEK WE DON'T REMEMBER OUR NAMES

Ash blushed as the person opposite caught a glimpse of the massive marker pen scrawl. She was forced to pencil the proposed plans into what tiny space Han had allowed her.

Another time, she was sitting with her family, planning a birthday party for the youngest, when she turned the page:

GET LAID
GET LAID
GET LAID

Across the whole weekend.

Ash snapped the book shut before anyone could see.

When it came to sex and relationships this was one of the areas they'd been raised most differently.

Ash asked Han to stop:

'You know what they're like about that stuff.'
'Oh fuck off, Ash, it's just a joke.'

Ash had wanted to speak but rolled a cigarette instead. She felt the paper listen to her lips, as it formed the right shape.

Han wouldn't let it drop.

'You take yourself too seriously.
You need to loosen up. And your family too.'

Han didn't see the flicker of agony in Ash's eyes as the words 'and your family too' gathered like a snowball in her mind.

And what do snowballs do?
They get bigger and bigger, as they acquire snow and ice,
Lodged in a heart, colder and more capable of causing damage, with time.

And your family too

And your family too
And your family too

Han didn't notice because she was busy writing 'PICK UP A SENSE OF HUMOUR' on the pages marked To Do

The waitress returns with a drink for Ash.

'Sorry about what I said before, I'm sure your mate has good reason.'
'She doesn't.'

A silence hangs, not an awkward one, but a potent one. The waitress tries again.

'I do this thing that might help. When I'm having a bad day, I split the day into sections.'
'How many sections'
'It depends.'

Ash really feels this waitress is onto something:
Because, yes, without a doubt it's true that sometimes you can have the most awful eleven til three, but then somewhere between 9 and 10 p.m. everything could be good again.

'Sooo, are you gonna order any food?'

Ash reads the name tag on her shirt and says,

'Yes, Taffy! I am. Thank you'.

The first time Ash and Han had come to this restaurant it was after their first autumn apart in three years. They were graduates now out in the world, or, trying to be.

Ash had ordered a salad and Han didn't like that.

'What? Are you worried about getting fat?'

Ash put the comment aside because she didn't want to get into it, didn't want to get into 'I'm more likely to have high blood pressure and diabetes than you',
And 'I'm more likely to be overlooked by the doctors than you',
And 'you know what I am actually allowed to order different food.'
She didn't want to get into it, because she didn't want to spoil the mood,
because actually, Ash had some really exciting news.

Just as she was about to –
            Han got there first.

Han had a looooot to talk about.
            She talked and talked about the places she'd been, the people she'd met.
Ash sat slightly distracted, trying to listen, trying to act like this was new information and not what Han had spent months posting on Insta in, practically, a live stream.

            'What have you been doing though, Ash?'
            'Applying for jobs mostly!'
            'Oh right, really living the dream.'

There was already such an exacting harshness, such a judgement, in the way Han had said it. But it was her little laugh afterwards that really made it hurt.

So Ash put her news away.

And instead kept Han talking.

There's a lot of debate about how many repetitions it takes to form a habit. And in this case Ash can't be sure. She swears Han wasn't always like this, but maybe she just didn't see it before.

Whether she was joyful or maudlin – just like that – it became Han the performer and Ash the audience.
Ash was always expected to be the model confidant.
Somehow their dynamic summed up in the fact Ash never got to choose the restaurant.

Ash became the board Han sounded all her feelings on.
Every thought of Han's offloaded,
without consideration or patience,

        chopped
        like onions across the table between them.

Ash would walk away eyes stinging, heart pounding, unaligned, drained, worried, and unheard.

      Most of all unheard.
      Always unheard.

And now as she looks back at the waitress, she thinks, maybe it had always been like this?
Because,

actually,

the reason they didn't debrief after nights out was:

'Come on, we're moving on!'
'What you on about? We only just got in! I only just got a drink!'
'Don't worry about it, I'll get you another one.'
'But it's banging here?'
'Yeah but. . .'

And Han would gesture towards the pair of new eyes she'd just met.

And, yeah, Ash thinks, staring back at the waitress, it had always been like this.

So she orders the grilled seabass with a side of rocket and chunky chips.
Because it's Friday, right?
And it's her first day off in months, so she might as well enjoy it.

Out on the street someone plays a saxophone version of a UK garage classic, and Ash doesn't even have energy to be nostalgic.

Ash knows, now, the reason she can't remember when exactly the balance tipped is because a balance had never truly been established. Han had cherished each minute with Ash the way children cherished sweets.

But not sweets offered.
More like: sweets cascading from a recently smashed pinata.
Han would always greedily take the best of Ash, with no regard for how depleted it might leave her.

The food comes and Ash eats it slowly, carefully.
Savours it.
She snorts at the gifs her sisters have sent in the group chat.
And she replies to a 'how was the interview?' message from her dad.
She's come to understand their overbearing love,
and she feels stronger knowing they've all got her back.

She places her phone down and watches the world waltz past.
So much of her life has been with Han
but at the same time so much of it hasn't,
because so much of it she'd held back. Because so much of it she couldn't be bothered to explain to Han who never listened and never sought to understand.

> You need to loosen up and your family too
> You need to loosen up and your family too
> You need to loosen up and your family too

Taffy comes over a couple more times and they chat. They talk about the restaurant and the people-watching potential. They talk about a high profile celebrity who always orders the same thing.

'Has your mate still not texted you?'
'No, she has. She's "on her way". She's just used to me waiting,

however long she takes.'

'Right. Sounds healthy.'

'Do you ever think about the word "waitress"?'

'In what sense?'

'It's like you're The Hostess of The Wait. At least, you have been today. It's like you're the compere of a shit comedy show where the last act won't turn up. The drums keep rolling but that last act just isn't stepping up.'

Taffy laughs and laughs and something about her draws Ash in, makes her laugh too, makes her feel validated and vindicated, even manages to make her see the funny side of the afternoon. And in that way that we get good – really, astonishingly good – at making friends when we're older, Ash and Taffy swap numbers. Within months they will have formed a friendship that will change both their lives, and they'll have just as many conversations that will make them laugh-cry about things like, 'Yeah but you know when you take hair vitamins, do you not worry that it will just be your pubes that grow out of control while your head goes bald?' as they will have conversations about the ways the world works and who the world works for. And neither will have to explain the context of their thoughts because they implicitly understand each other and each other's lives.

But for now, carefully, Ash asks:

'If you were me, what would you say?'

'Don't ask me that! I have a feeling I'm waaaay harsher than you.'

'I've written "Don't worry about it, let's rain check, I've

got plans this afternoon".'

'That's actually quite good. . . do you have plans this after-noon?'

'No, it's just time to call it now, right?'

'Yeah, I think it is.'

For dessert, Taffy recommends the mango cheesecake.

It arrives as a perfect circle, a firm base, a smooth top: sweet. Ash requests a teaspoon instead of a fork so she can make this moment last.

As she swallows, it's hazy but it's there, this memory of her first meeting with Han. Of Han holding up the class. Of knowing imme-diately how much they didn't relate. Because Han had walked in waving her free pass.

One had stayed the same.
The other, changed.

Rey Goes on a Journey

As a child Rey had learnt to spell her mum's name, Feride, before she learnt to spell her own.

Her own – Reyhan – had confused her – the 'E' that sounded like an English 'A' and then the actual 'A' which sounded like an English 'U'.
A soup of confused vowels.

When people asked her name she'd mumble it timidly, with an upward inflection at the end.
Offering it like an apology.

People would raise their eyebrows and shake their heads as if to say, 'Odd child. . . doesn't seem to know her own name.'

Mrs Farooq had tried to help her suggesting Rey explain it like this,

'Rey like day and -han like Honey'

Rey would nod, trying to take the information on board,
Still, the fact remained she never felt confident in her name, but
she did feel confident with:

F   E   R   I   D   E

Feride she could grasp at like trusted building blocks.
She felt certain with those letters.
She would sound them out.
Would feel the syllables through.

FEH RIH DEH
or
FERRRRYYYYY DEHHH

She was able to correct any mispronunciation with ease.

While her classmates addressed their cards to 'Mummy'
their little 'm's joined up and curly,
Rey would write her mum's actual name.

She relished the solidity and strength of what it felt like to write
that name.
Every single letter of 'Feride' has a line,
a backbone,
a spine.

'It means one of a kind.'
Rey would chime.
As she lingered lovingly, over the dot above the i.

Taking her time to draw a circle which, to her, felt like an eye above
the world. An eye looking out for everything and everyone.

As soon as she was old enough to make such a request, Reyhan
introduced herself to everyone as Rey.
Reyhan took too much explaining, Rey was easy.
Though sometimes even Rey gets spelt wrong.
Rei.
And that spelling makes her happy, makes her feel more like her
mum
because she gets a dot on the i too.

Her love for language – a love she indulged in over a decade of
higher education –
Started with her mother.
Because when Rey was born, Feride had only been in the country
a year or two longer than her,
Rey and Feride, daughter and mother,
learnt their English together,
pretty much in tandem, pretty much at the same rate.

This meant they both jumbled things in specific, often comedic
ways.

Rey remembers being aged seven or maybe eight,
And after too long of a particular conundrum playing on her mind

she looked up and asked her teacher, Mrs Farooq (who could always be heard traversing the tables of the classroom, not because of her steps but the jingle jangle of her thousand bangles)

'Mrs Farooq – sorry but why do we say, 'brown new' even if it's not brown?'

Mrs Farooq, who had been learning Rey's quirks and knew something of them personally herself too, took a moment to comprehend. Asking the small mind bursting with two tongues:,

'No need to be sorry! Hmm I'm not sure, can you use it for me in a sentence, Rey?'

'This car is brown new. . .?'

Mrs Farooq smiled with the firm kindness all primary school teachers tend to be born with and stated,

'Ah, I see. It's not 'brown' – it's 'brand new', Rey. Which means really, really new. Fresh from the factory.'

Rey absorbed the information carefully. She would have to go home and explain this to her mum. Alongside the fact the word comes straight from the horse's mouth, not the horse's house.

At the end of the year, they gifted Mrs Farooq a box of fresh baklava so huge she enjoyed it with her own family for nearly a week.

Primary school teachers meet child after child on a never-ending carousel of differing needs but Reyhan only had the one Mrs Farooq and so she thinks of her often.

Rey has written (in one of the many pieces of writing she's still not brave enough to submit to any magazines) that language can never be used incorrectly,
only differently.
She's written that
ultimately language breathes, has a life of its own,
and so we must let the language live.
Language exists outside of the ordinary
and morphs like a chameleon through the tongues of many.
though there's always someone trying to keep the gates,
language is a thing that will always escape.
Language will streak naked across fields of logic.
Of course it can be displaced,
and, certainly, it can be muddled,
but those muddles must always be met with compassion.

The memory of Mrs Farooq's bangles linger in Rey's mind every time she types, filling the space between the lines. And now as she sits on the edge of an island, on a high-backed stool, in the centre of her friend Kara's kitchen, she says,

'I cut my tickets last night.'

'You did what?' responds Kara.

'Oh, errr, in Turkish we'd say "kestim biletti", which means "I booked the tickets".'

But

        translates as
      "I cut the tickets".'

Rey starts to apologise but Kara raises a fond palm.

      'Why are you apologising? Carry on! When are you off?
      And where!?'

      'I've not been back to the place my mum was born since
      the year my mum died.'

Rey does try to say this breezily, but as far as statements go, this one's a storm. A sense of 'ohmygod I'm actually going to do this?!' mists her face before the sentence is fully out.

Kara mirrors her inhale of breath and in an outward flow says,

      'It's going to be okay.'

In a way that also says,

'It's okay to say you hear her voice all the time.
It's okay that the thought of moving on scares you because it feels too much like forgetting.
It's okay the house is still full of the boxes you haven't unpacked since moving back.
It's okay that you feel all these feelings. It's okay, Rey.'

Kara holds the look in Rey's eye like it's play dough. Like it's something she can shape. Just as she's about to go on she feels a poke in the leg.

'Mummy? Can I have BIKKETS?'

Kara reaches for the tin so her daughter's ten dinky fingers can delve in, grab a custard cream for herself, for her mum and thrust one at Rey too.

Rey accepts the bikket, ignoring the faint taste of craft glue.

They dunk and talk and dunk and talk and dunk and talk,
About hand luggage and passports
and *make sure you measure your bag even though I swear whenever I get on a plane everyone's version of cabin friendly is twice the size of mine and apparently totally fine.*

There are further discussions to be had but friendship is knowing the time isn't always now.
But be ready for when the time does come.
Because the time always does.

*

As Rey boards the plane to Cyprus she replays the moments which took her to this present moment.

When clearing out the Brighton flat ahead of her return to London she'd found, tucked away in almost every drawer, photo after photo.

A life Rey had chosen not to think about, found its way back to her
Reminding her.
Her mum had worn soft denim jackets and sandals on the beach,
Her mum had changed hair colour in accordance with the fashions,
her mum had sipped cocktails,
and stood in front of holiday destinations,
her mum had ridden on water flumes and shrieked as the water
splashed her face.
She'd blown out candles with Rey on her knee,
and thrown her the sweetest of sixteenths.
She'd cooked meals,
and popped champagne corks, baked cakes, pastries, pies.

Somehow Rey had forgotten that Feride, once upon a time, had
been alive.

It had started to feel that keeping her grief a secret had meant keeping her mum a secret too.
So she started to post the pictures online.

And to one particular image, a cousin replied:

> Omg look at u cuzin & omgggg look at me?! Typical. . . we
> posing while ur mums playing in sand behind us. I remem-
> ber that day – do u? Your dad forgot matches for mangal!
> He kept saying sorry and teyze was telling him off – she
> always say don't apologise! Ohhh such sweet memories,
> happy you shared this! xxxx

The tears streaming from the laughing eyes emoji felt apt.
Rey didn't remember this day at all, and the fact she didn't set a wheel in motion,
a wheel that moved her to book this flight across these oceans
because there are stories she hasn't heard
and people who remember so much more.

When they land in Cyprus all the passengers clap,
and as she grabs her bag from overhead Rey is reminded there's no covered walkway to ease her from plane to port.
There's only a sudden shift.
The marked lift in temperature,
the smell of hot tarmac
and a heat she can taste.
There's the feeling of all the lights in the world being turned on
and the realisation of how dim London light really is.
It ignites a mixture of familiarity and awe.
It is immediate and irreplicable.
The warmth feels like a hug but also unrelentingly raw.
Rey wonders if her mum felt this too and if she felt it every time.
And how she coped.

Before she treads the metal steps she turns and hugs the lady who was in the seat next to her.
Early seventies, short haircut, gold earrings sagging, burgundy lip liner, a touch of eyeshadow.
A cheekiness in her eyes.
The kind of woman who is widowed, unfrightened of being alone, family spread wide,
Forever catching flights.

Jumping on planes to and from Cyprus the way one might hop on
a bus from Lewisham to Peckham.
(Which incidentally Rey has been doing visiting friends frequently.)
They'd talked through four of the five hour flight.
Much ground covered and mutual acquaintances discovered.
Small island Cyprus, big hearts.
The lady wishes Rey good luck.
And means it with all the breath in her chest.
She air kisses Rey on both cheeks and as she pulls back says,
'My love, in the end it's all just kismet'.

Clutching her carrier bag full of chocolate gifts for the family Rey
blinks and feels the flash of this same journey from another time.
When Rey was around six years old,
the year Rey's father had died.

On that flight, Rey had asked over and over, 'Muuuuumm, will
Dad be there? Are we going to Baba?' And every time she said it
Feride's eyes had welled up.
The first language they spoke was Turkish,
the second English,
the third was the words they spoke in tears.
In sobs.
Finally, Feride had said,

'I told you, didn't I? My love? That he's up in the sky now and he's
not coming back down but he's watching over us all the time.'

Rey's eyes had brightened with the undefeatable energy that only
small children can really muster.

'Were we just with him then?'

Feride paused, knowing, as she'd known the last few months, that everything she said to this child would now stay with her forever. All her words had weight now.
And while she'd once shared that responsibility with her partner, it was all up to her now.
'We were,' she confirmed. Looking up, assigning the sky
a forever-friend to her daughter.

So it follows that, Rey, a lifetime later,
turns back and looks at the expanse of blue one last time before she enters the airport.
Feeling strongly that it, that they, carried her here.
She thinks of the eye above her mother's name,
that eye above the world,
the eye on a silver chain around her neck.
She thinks of her father,
and she thinks of the Turkish word for sky: gökyüzü.
Which translates crudely to something like: the sky's face.
And it's true they are both up there now.
All eyes on her.

When she finally shuffles into the arrivals lounge her cousin blurts out,

'My God! You could be your mother!'

Rey remembers standing in this spot as Feride's own cousin had greeted her all those years ago. She remembers being scooped up into the warm embrace of someone with a soon to be familiar face. She remembers her mum collapsing into her own cousin's arms and wailing that her husband had been taken far too young.

The airport with all its coming and goings, all its goodbyes and hellos reminds Rey, polished tile by polished tile, that loss has always been such a big part of her life.

Unlike her mother she couldn't cave into her cousin's arms, not yet.

But they hug and it does feel like hope. The cousin, Yıldız – no dots above the I, but ironically meaning 'Star' which absolutely does live up high – has been messaging Rey for weeks.

'Stay as long as you want.'
'Of course I'll get you from the airport.'
'I'll take time off work, so we can spend some time together.'
'Go on some trips?'
'Remind me, are you still vegetarian?'

In the car, as she drives them from airport to village,
they stop to let a herd of sheep pass and take their rightful charge of the road
As the sheep murmur and bleat, Yıldız reiterates,
'We can drive wherever you want, hayatım, drive wherever you need.'

Yıldız makes the suggestion as though it's been sitting on the starting block of her tongue for decades, just waiting for permission to go.

'hayatım,' Rey's favourite of the pet names. Not satisfied with 'my love,' people say instead 'my hayat.' My life. The air I breathe. The thing that sustains me.

Within hours of arriving at the village the house is bustling with guests.
family, neighbours, friends, some people counting as all three.

The thing about small islands is that they feel grief collectively.
Community is woven into their tapestry.
What happens to one, happens to all,
so they come to the door to greet Rey
with food, savoury and sweet,
and they kiss her on each cheek.

Rey, to her surprise, becomes quickly accustomed to the way they talk about death.
She laughs to herself, it's almost the way people in England talk about the weather.
The rhythm goes:
Start with a wallowing, which builds to a cacophony of everyone's two cents and then the last phrase,
'Eh. What can we do?'
And it's true, not much can be done.

When Feride died, the London contingent of her family took charge.
They filled the house with food and chatter.
With börek. With more börek than Rey had ever seen.
They took charge of all the important conversations, organised all that needed organising.

Took care of all practicalities

Doused Rey's palms with rose water.

Rey feels now that she owes them so much for taking over.

She knows they organised everything, in the hope that she would organise herself.

The three nights after the funeral are hazy in her mind.

She still feels the fullness of each gathering.

The women in one room, scarves concealing hair regardless of creed, everyone just doing the respectful thing, For Feride, who was loved, so loved.

The men in the other room,

The Hoca singing low: sweet and sad the prayers and songs switching seamlessly between ancient and recent tongues

And then the bustling communal feasting.

Recipes shared,

soup sipped,

semolina stirred. Then the forty-day gap. Then the last goodbye.

Rey, being Rey, picked up more and more language each and every time.

Rey, being Rey, thought and thought about the etymology, the meaning.

Cousins of cousins of cousins observed her as she seemingly observed barely anything at all.

*

Every morning the chickens wake Rey up,

and she worries she'll return to London barely rested at all,

but then the prayers play five times a day.
and the prayers take her breath away.
Five times a day she feels safe,
because five times a day she's reminded of her place,
her smallness in this huge world full of mystery.
She's not a religious person,
but she is a spiritual one.
The fact there are things that none of us know fills her with absolute relief.

So just like everyone else she stops mid-sentence to listen as the prayers float on the breeze,
into every cranny and every nook.
Because believer or not, this minute is a welcome resting spot
Where all Rey has to do is be.

Rey thinks about how it's never ever silent here.
If it's not talk and the creaking bones of emphatic gesticulation,
it's the trees speaking instead,
or the cattle's beating heart, listening to the weather as it plans
what to do next.

*

After a few days of settling in, Rey and Yıldız visit her father's mum.
People had always talked about his mother's pomegranates,
known across the island,
her tree the most abundant for miles.
As they pull up to the house the trees stand tall, stand regal,
older than them all.

From now on Rey will never ever come to this country without visiting this tree.
Not now she's been told it's the tree under which her parents shared secret kisses.

Secret kisses everyone knew about.

Rey and Yıldız peck the elderly lady's hand and tap it to their forehead,
bowing to her in respect.
They treat her with all the majesty she deserves but they know, too, inside she's still a spritely girl.
On an up-turned steel bucket fashioned into a table is a basket brimming with pomegranates, grapefruits and mandarins,
all picked this morning ready for them to take home.
She doesn't have much to give her granddaughters.
But she does have this.

They know it will have been her, almost a century old, who climbed the rickety ladder and pulled the fruit down. They know she won't have been careful. And they know she'll spit venom if they attempt to tell her off for doing something like that at *her* age.

So instead they coo in gratitude and allow their mouths to water.

Everything here tastes better. When Rey returns to London, for weeks, tomatoes will brutally disappoint her. Feride especially always moaned about this, she had loved the world they'd built in London but there was so much she missed about Cyprus too. And this was somehow always encapsulated by dissatisfied bites into watery fruit.

So Rey eats everything her grandma offers her.
In the kitchen Rey first held life in.
Her grandma had once placed a fluffy yellow bundle into her hands and told to her to be gentle.
Feride had stroked Rey's hair and told her,
'You must always be this gentle, Rey, always be this soft.'

Her grandma looks at grown-up Rey and cherishes seeing the family eyes looking back at her.

Her grandma recalls a memory from a long time ago. She sees herself sat in this, her beloved kitchen, getting ready to snap the neck of a chicken. How she always did – before Feride pleaded 'Not in front of Rey, she'll cry about that for days'. It was one of the few times in her life she'd complied – when she felt in herself she shouldn't have. Maybe Rey would be a little more robust if she'd been afforded a little more reality.

*

On the beach Rey takes a sip of fresh, cold, sweet-sour lemonade and poses a question to Yıldız.

'Do you ever think about how much the Turkish love to label?'
'What you mean?'
'Well, in English, it's aunty and uncle and that's it.'
'Ahaaa, but in Turkish it's amca for Dad's brother and dayı for

Mum's brother.'

'Maybe because it makes it easier to talk behind each other's backs.
. . fewer crossed wires!'

'Crossed wires. . .' Yıldız looks embarrassed – her English doesn't
stretch this far. 'What does that mean?'

Rey remembers Mrs Farooq and responds accordingly.

Before Yıldız can expand on what she's learnt, a raindrop lands on
her nose and then another and then another. The sky clouds over
and the water stills. Yıldız smiles the smile Rey is dreading leaving
at the airport. She grabs Rey's hand and leads her running into the
sea. The sand parts for them and they howl with laughter as the
rain hammers down.

And then the all-body laughter, turn to all body tears.

Rey looks up at the sky and cries.

For the first time in years, lets tears fall as the rain does.

She cries now because she never once cried at the doctor's appoint-
ments where again and again she had to make sure her mum
completely understood the diagnosis.

She cries now because she never once dared cry in front of Mel.

She cries now because she has not just Yıldız in her life now but
Yıldız's father, her dad's big brother.

She cries because – internally always, wherever she is – she feels
both home and away.

She cries now because tears had always been a third language to her,
but for a long time she hasn't allowed her feelings to have their say.

She cries and cries until all her tears are drained.

And then calmly, quietly, Rey asks to go home.

In the shower she combs the jasmine-scented conditioner Lainey recommended to her through her hair, she replays one of the stories her grandmother had told her last week. She patches the words together and imagines it like this:

The toilet, back then, had been at the end of the garden. She does remember that – that awful toilet!
Rey feeling bold – she'd held a whole chick in her hands that day, after all – insisted on going alone.
Just as Rey reached the most jagged steps,
the defeated hum of all the electricity for miles around grinding to a halt was heard.
The neighbours, outside in their gardens, gossiping through the vines, immediately started to bicker:
'I'm telling you; you do have my torch! I lent it to you last summer.'
In the hubbub a small crash and a squeal was heard.
And then ceaseless sobs and then: 'MUUUM!'

'Stay still my love,' bellowed Feride with a volume that caught half the village off guard.

A lilt of panic found its way into the neighbours usually unphase-able voice too
because there were the sharp edges of the chicken wire,
and there was that stark drop at the end of the garden,
and there was a small girl from London in an entirely unrecognisable situation.

Feride thundered through the house searching for candles and matches.

She knocked a plate over.

As it smashed the neighbours reassured her, 'Don't worry, a breakage is good luck!'

As she was searching bizarre places, where the matches categorically would not be.

Frantically, senselessly, opening and closing the fridge.

'Rey's not like us. She didn't grow up like we did, she doesn't know anything like this.'

But then: down, way down, at the end of the garden a small brightly coloured glow was seen,

Tiny spotlights of colour emanating from two tiny feet.

Rey had remembered that her new trainers lit up,

all she had to do was kick.

It wasn't enough light to really move anywhere,

but just enough light that she could check there were no animals in the immediate vicinity

and just enough light that she could squat her legs and wee.

I must have been so proud of myself thinks Rey as Yıldız knocks on the door.

'Rey, are you okay in there? You've been ages. Don't forget the water will run out!'

'I'm coming, don't worry! Let me get dressed!'

When she returns to the kitchen her cousin is crouched over a large wicker basket, liberating black-eyed beans from their shells, for dinner.

Rey loves to say the phrase 'kolay gelsin,' and regrets that in English there aren't phrases like this. Phrases for when someone is working hard. No one stops to say, 'I hope this work comes easy to you'. So while in Cyprus, Rey says it as often as she can, to everyone doing anything.

In return Yıldız wishes her good health.

'Thank you for today,' says Rey.

before taking a deep breath, and finally, collapsing into her cousin's arms.

Yıldız sighs, her own tears – the ones she felt she didn't have a right to cry earlier in the sea – begin to fall and Rey feels held. She doesn't need to say or do anything. All she has to do is let herself be held.

Later, as the sun sets, they drag bread through olive oil, sip wine and talk about when Yıldız should next come to London. Rey makes a firm case for the autumn because that's when the UK is at its most beautiful, and because the autumn is soon.

On her last night, Rey sits out in the garden with a notebook she purchased and a scrawly pen. She describes in meticulously chosen words every single thing she can see and hear. It was an exercise

Yıldız suggested, to help her feel more present. Yıldız's father has come to see her off but is happy to let the women sit and do their own thing. He's a quiet man himself.

Rey turns to Yıldız who is persevering with the book of poetry Rey gifted her on the first night and says,

> 'What's that smell though?'
> 'Which one?'
> 'I don't know. . . I swear it's more prominent at night. . . Citrussy, fresh.'

Yıldız gestures towards a particular potted plant, leaves bountiful and shaped like tongues.

Rey gets down on her knees and inhales.

> 'Yessss it's this one. It's definitely this one.
> What is it?'

The uncle looks up and exchanges a look with his daughter before saying to Rey:

> 'It's Reyhan.'
> 'It's what?'
> 'It's Reyhan. It's a type of sweet native basil. Your mum's favourite smell, she always said the scent took her home, no matter where she was. She used to press it into the pages of her books.'

Rey takes a piece in her hand, feels its smooth texture and presses it into the pages.

*

In the morning the plane lifts off and Rey feels herself back in her parents' grasp. She thinks, it's funny.
With all that curiosity for language.
It had never occurred to her to look up her own name.

A Wedding
in Full Swing

So that's a year of preparation playing out.
Several mood boards reflecting several cultures coming together
in real life.
Not just for the day, but forever.
Time spent getting the right kind of drums and enough musicians
to meet the brief,
and food that will please everyone
(an impossible task, but worth a try).
Carefully deciding which curses to break
and which traditions to honour.
There's been a lot on the couples' shoulders.
A wedding is big thing, a really big thing.

Ash has been looking forward to this for months
because this is the first time Ash has been invited to a wedding

entirely alone
acutely aware of the way adulthood tends to strip us of firsts,
she savours them every time.

Frustratingly, the cabbie made her late.
But she remains hopeful for an amazing night,
a woman full of hope: one of the more beautiful things in this life.
She strides now up the gravel drive,
past groomsmen posing with man buns and cigars in their mouths.
Past an older lady calming a hot flush by the open door.
Past the photographer's assistant polishing a lens,
and into the foyer
where she's met by the seating plan,
She steps through the main door and into the hall.

And oh. . .

Oh, it's more gorgeous than she'd imagined.

More magical.

Completely disarming.

In a way, she wishes the cabbie was still here so he could eat
his words,
because nothing here is 'typical'.
Because yes, it's a manor house
but it feels lived in.
Floor lovingly tarnished by centuries of dancing.

Ash swoons at the autumnal leaves scattered like lipstick kisses
across every table,
lit by the flickering flames of a thousand candles.
And there in the middle,
centre of the dancefloor:
The couple.
THE couple.
Dil dancing in worship of the DJ in his DJ booth,
Gard in a burnt orange suit,
Dil in a white silk slip dress,
tattooed shoulders.
Thigh slit.
Ugh, iconic, thinks Ash.

When she spots her table, she attempts to assess the circle of
strangers from afar.
Please be fun, she thinks, please be fun, please be fun.
(She says it three times for optimum luck.)
She sees her empty chair waiting.
On one side, a woman is trying to hide tears as she rifles through
her gold clutch.
On the other, a woman with an elegant chignon and a midnight
blue dress is smiling wistfully.
Weddings bring everything up thinks Ash, knowingly.

'Hi, hi my name is Ash, lovely to meet you all.'

A woman called Reyhan, 'but call me Rey for short', to her left,
and a woman called Hatty to her right.

Commands are spoken into headsets,

glasses are topped up.

Three delectable courses of food, loudly enjoyed.

And just as hundreds of dessert spoons are licked to gleaming

and all the bellies are full

and all the faces are glowing,

the satisfaction of a really memorable meal.

Just, just, *just* as everyone would quite like to slip out of their fancy clothes

and take a lovely food-filled nap,

the music shifts

and attention turns to the top table.

Gard stands up,

walks his wife to the dancefloor

For a first dance.

To an *incredibly* sexually explicit song.

This makes Clea, a few tables over and dressed in floor length crimson, laugh,

because of course her big brother would choose this song.

Oh Gard, she says to herself, you and your rebel heart.

She rises from her chair to clap,

moves her hips in an infinity motion to the beat,

wondering if she'll find a rebel girl of her own.

Where are you, she yearns to know, where and when will we meet?

Back at table nine, Hatty fares less well,

bursts into tears.

Ash and Rey look at each other in that way that women often do.

A look that says,

'Assemble! Let's get to the bottom of this.'
And Hatty – even though she promised herself she wouldn't -
tells them all about Al
About the way she never replied to his text and hasn't heard from
him since.

In the toilets, two teenage girls talk enthusiastically about a podcast
they've both been listening to,
'I am *obsessed* with Dia.'

Outside, numbers are exchanged for the first time.

There will be first kisses tonight.

Somewhere else old flames pretend they're not unsettled to see
each other again,
exchange pleasantries and walk away.

There will also be closure tonight.

In the queue for the photobooth a woman called Magenta and her
daughter Ruby rifle through the props box, encouraging others to
do the same.
Magenta goes for a pair of comedy glasses.
And Ruby a feather boa.
They practice poses, besides themselves with laughter.

Dil and Gard dance like they've known each other forever
and someone says, 'It's funny; they haven't been together long.'
Someone else replies, 'Yeah but when you know you know, and

Dil has a strong head on her shoulders she knows what she wants.'

A glass is tapped with a spoon.
And then tapped again.
The groomsmen roar.
The bridesmaids cheer.
Seats are hurried to.
A man stands up.
Ash barely concentrates on his words,
because she's thinking so much more about what to say to Hatty.
She knows in some people's version of her own story she could be
accused of cutting ties too suddenly.
Too out of the blue.
Cold!
And after all those years?
How could you?
But Ash regrets nothing,
Because Han was only ever there for a good time.
Whenever Ash needed her to step up,
grow up,
or show up,
she didn't.

Ash looks to Hatty and says
                'You'll be okay, sis.'

There's something so powerful about women who aren't related,
calling each other sister.
It soothes a wound you didn't know you had.
Allows the missing parts of the puzzle to land.

Offers a belonging.

It's a love you don't have to give but choose to.

It's a reminder from woman to woman, that we are compasses to each other.

'Ash is right. You will,' concurs Rey.

And then the three of them return their ears to the speeches.

There's not much more for them to say.

Things to feel, of course.

Infinitely.

To the moon and back, deeply.

But to actually say? There's not much left.

Rey finds herself invested in the stories about Dil and Gard.

(And not just because the best man is very, very handsome.)

The detangling of Gard's broken heart

and all the ways Dil was the only woman who could.

As a finale Dil's mum raises a glass and says,

'It's all written in the stars.'

Rey wonders if it really is all just kismet, as the lady on the plane had said.

She trusts herself enough to turn to Hatty and say:

'When my mum died I learnt how much we can't control. You can't make this guy be with you. But you do have to be with yourself, day in, day out. So why not make that the love affair of your life? Choose that commitment instead. Choose you. You are the only constant. Everything else is out of your hands, So make the most of choosing you. That's what I'm trying to do'

'Oooffff cheers to that' says Ash raising her glass before sending her mum a message:

Sorry I was such a cow about the dishwasher this morning, love you loads, can't wait to tell you about this wedding xxx

The three women look at each other.
It's like they've known each other forever
from some unknown before.
'Girls?' says Ash.
'Yeah?' They both say feeling the weight of everything in their hearts.
'You know what we need right now? We need to be dancing, come on get up.'
And this is probably the greatest idea anyone has ever had.

The three of them check each other's lipstick,
take a sip of orange,
initially sticking to the outskirts of the dancefloor,
before collectively agreeing to dive into the middle
Dollar bills sticking to their heels.
The floor bouncing beneath them.
Songs they know
and songs they don't.
Dil shimmies over and kisses them all on both cheeks.

'Thank you so much for coming! You're all staying here tonight
as well, yes? See you at breakfast, right?'

And with that Ash, Hatty and Rey know they will stay up all night.
They will be the last to leave the dance floor
and as daylight breaks, they'll sneak around the grounds,
sit on the edge of the water fountain,
throw wishes over their backs and into the water.
Will share more about themselves than they thought they could.
And they will love telling the story forever, of how they met.

But first the cake!
Which makes Rey think of Mel,
and how one time,
Before she'd had a chance to bemoan her carrot cake arriving clad
in cream cheese,
Mel had swapped their plates, so she could eat his lemon instead.
There was so much he didn't know about her, but he did, at least,
know that.
And that's enough.
She looks out now and sees new chapters being written,
can't wait for Yıldız to fly in next week.
She's been thinking about what she wants with her life.
And why.
But for now she just wants this moment.
For now she just wants this music.
This night.
This sense of the past meeting the future.

When the music is lowered, she's worried the night is over.
She's heady, the right side of tipsy.
spinning slightly as the crowd is herded outside.
The crisp cold night waking her skin.

She chuckles to herself.
Ash hears and then Hatty too
and then they are all, mindlessly,
passing the chuckle from one to the other.
It's nice to be standing there among three hundred people all on
the same wave.
This is nice.
This is really *fucking nice*, thinks Rey.

In someone's pocket a missing box of matches have emerged.
And then the whistle of a lit firework is heard.
Colours and sparks crusade through the sky
Crackling up up and up into the night.
On instinct: Rey cries.
Just gently,
just warmly,
tears tricking.
Because, 'There you both are,' she whispers to herself.
Mouthing a hello to her mum and dad in the sky,
she feels an emotion she can't identify.
It's similar to acceptance, but not quite.
There's probably a word for it somewhere.
And maybe one day she'll find it.
Next week she will start to write it.

But for now, everyone goes inside
and Rey decides to stay outside a moment longer.
Just to breathe,
just to be.
She lets the breeze dry her tears,
tells herself it's a kiss from her parents on each cheek.
She lets herself smile.
blows them a kiss back.

Inside, Hatty is deleting all the texts in her drafts folder.
Clea is flirting with someone in the band before the music starts
back up.
And, outside, Rey makes a promise.

As she returns inside, she notices a mum slipping her kids into their
pyjamas.
The husband says, 'That really was a good idea.'
Rey concurs.

   '*Really* good idea.'

All the girls on the dancefloor have kicked off their heels.
Rey loosens her hair, Lainey did a beautiful job, but she needs to
feel free.
Back at the table she devours the salted-caramel cake waiting for
her.
Hatty confesses she was tempted to eat Rey's and claim her portion
had never come.
Rey realises she's taken barely any photos so grabs her new friends

for a selfie. She sends it to Sal.

Who instantly replies:

GORGEOUS! ARE THERE ANY SEXY MEN?

She ponders this.

Will come back to that in the morning.

The night is young after all.

She can't yet say for certain.

But for now, it's dancing.

And the seasons changing.

Leaves orange and red as they say goodbye.

Beautiful as they end.

And new friends.

New doors opening.

Old bonds strengthening.

And maybe soon some loving.

It's not the life she expected,

most certainly not the one she would have chosen.

But it's hers now.

And she will love it.

Because how dare she not?

As long as she's here, she's lucky.

For the first time in a long time,

she knows she'll be alright.

Maybe even brilliant.

Ash taps her on the shoulder and says, 'Okay, sis?'

That little word again.

She looks around.

She sees all the women she knows

All the women she is still to know

And every day she learns more about all the woman she is.

Acknowledgements

Firstly, thank YOU. Thank you for buying books – in doing so you keep a million dreams alive. Thank you for taking the time to read mine, and thank you for allowing my girls into your world. I hope you love them as much as I do.

Thank you to my family. My mum especially – one way or another, you always nurtured the artist in me: the little plastic table in the corner of the salon and the notebooks always waiting in the Christmas stocking. Thank you for asking so many times, 'Tuts! Why don't you write a book?' Thank you, Dad, for keeping the fruit bowl full of pomegranates while I was writing.

Thank you to my friends. You know who you are. I'm grateful for tequila on Tuesday afternoons, bouquets of flowers, stomps in the woods, long lunches where you asked me all the difficult questions, slow Sundays together and those voice notes telling me to keep going. Thank you for watering me.

Shout out to the many ladies of south east London who know me for the hairdryer in my hand as much as the pen. Your support and curiosity has always lit me up.

Abby and Bridie; thank you for everything you do for women writers at Dear Damsels. Thank you for seeing in me a writer you wanted to publish and holding my every idea with such delicacy.

Thank you Ellis Muddle for the front cover of dreams.

And lastly, because women never do this – not really – I'd like to thank myself. You did it, babes, you wrote a book. We don't always get to see names like our own on the cover and we don't always get to read characters like the women we know among us. What a cherished thing, cheers to that.

So Long As You Write:
Women on Writing

Why do you write? To record, to discover, to escape, to create?

Whatever the reason, when women put pen to paper, it is a way of sharing our words in a world where we are often made to feel our stories aren't worth being told.

In *So Long As You Write*, fifteen women writers explore what haappens when we give ourselves this space – whether it's the joy of opening a new notebook or the thrill of a new idea, or the self-doubt and uncertainty that those things can bring.

Edited by Kerry Ryan, founder of Write Like a Grrrl, this collection is the perfect place to turn for a reminder that it doesn't matter who is reading – so long as you write.

Tools for Surviving a Storm
by Nadia Henderson

In a transporting, original collection, Nadia Henderson examines the lines
between nature and the human world through stories set in landscapes
both brutal and beautiful.

Journeying from Sweden's ancient woods to the floodplains of the
American South, the women in these stories navigate loneliness, loss
and what it means to be alive in an ever-changing world.

What She's Having:
Stories of Women and Food

Food is about so much more than just the first bite . . .

What we eat can fill us up, satisfy our needs or leave us hungry for more.
It connects us to our culture, defines our routines and flavours our fondest memories.

Whole stories are made across a dinner table, and in *What She's Having*,
sixteen writers explore the complex and meaningful relationships that women
have with the food we cook, eat and share.

Bringing together fiction, non-fiction and poetry, this collection
of women's stories about food is something to savour.

**ALSO PUBLISHED
BY DEAR DAMSELS**

*Let Me Know When You're Home:
Stories of Female Friendship*

What is it that makes female friendship so special / complex / intense /
important / messy / supportive / essential?

From growing up together to growing apart, from the oldest of friends to
the fake ones, our relationships with other women can be our greatest loves.
They can also be difficult, elusive and the source of our deepest heartbreaks.

In *Let Me Know When You're Home*, fifteen women writers look at female friendship
in all its forms, in a collection of fiction, non-fiction and poetry that is
both a frank exploration of these relationships and a true celebration
of what women can achieve with the support of each other.

dear damsels
your words | your stories

deardamsels.com

⊙ deardamsels